MW01125685

PIPER DAVENPORT

Road To

ABSOLUTION

DOGS OF FIRE BOOK #3

2018 – 2ⁿᵈ Edition Piper Davenport
Cover Copyright 2019
All rights reserved.
Published in the United States

Sale of this book without a front cover may be unauthorized. If this book is coverless, it may have been reported to the publisher as "unsold or destroyed" and neither the author nor the publisher may have received payment for it.

Road to Absolution is a work of fiction. Names, characters, places, and incidents are the products of the author's imagination and are used fictitiously. Any resemblance to actual events, locales, or persons, living or dead, is entirely coincidental.

Cover Art
Jackson Jackson

Cover Models
Stock Images

ISBN-13: 9781705980941

For JBJ
I love you

ONE

Cassidy

Eight years ago…

"CARTER," I WHISPERED, forcing back tears. "I have to go."

"Why, Cass?" he demanded.

I stared up at my best friend and tried not to fold. "You're leaving—"

"I'll be back in less than a year."

Carter had driven to my place, rather than heading home after work, and he now stood in my kitchen (after sneaking in through my bedroom window), his face contorted in frustration as I tried to explain in person what I'd tried to explain over the phone. My parents were still at work and my sisters were out with their boyfriends, so I had the house to myself... which almost never happened.

"But if you're not here, there's no reason for me to stick around." I smiled. "Who knows where the Air Force will take you?"

He shook his head and ran his hands through his hair. "Damn it, Cass. I don't get this need you have to run."

I giggled. "You've known me since I was six. I have always wanted to run."

Carter Quinn had been my constant shadow ever since my parents moved me and my sisters to the property adjacent to the Quinn farm eleven years ago. It had started on my first day of first grade when he put a cockroach in my hair and I calmly removed it and named it "George." He was two years older than me, but ever since then, we'd spent pretty much every day together trekking through the wooded areas around our homes and lazy water "rides" on what he called the Quinn River. Of course, it was more of a pond, but it was safe to swim in and sometimes we would all take turns pushing each other in inner tubes in order to feel like we were all on some kind of rapids adventure. Silly kid stuff that I was going to miss.

"That's not what I meant," he grumbled.

"I know, buddy." I sighed, trying once again to bolster my resolve.

Carter was the fifth of six brothers, all rambunctious little boys who grew up to be gorgeous, strong, respectful men. They loved their Mama, and had a deep reverence for women in general, but that didn't mean they didn't take advantage of the fact they were all illegally good-looking.

"I can't believe you're giving up your senior year."

"To dance in *France*, Carter!" I said for the umpteenth time.

"You could dance in good old America," he said, also for the umpteenth time. "What if you hate Paris and I'm not here to help you pack up and come home?"

"You leave in a week." I rolled my eyes. "You won't be

2

back for at least eight months, probably longer, and then that'll be for what, a week or two? Then onto something else for another year or more, right? I'll do my year in Paris and beat you back here either way. It's the perfect chance for me to finish school and train with a prestigious ballet company… and take my mind off the fact that you're going to be flying planes into combat. It's a win-win."

He knew how much I hated school. I was never good with the politics of high school and once he left, I was bored… and a target.

"Are you still dealing with assholes?"

"Not since you forced your brother to stick close to me," I said with a sigh.

"I didn't force him to do anything. You know he thinks of you like the sister he never had."

I chuckled. "Or wanted."

Carter grinned. "Aidan adores you. Just don't let him know I told you."

Aidan was the baby of the family and one year younger than me, but you'd never know to look at him. He was six-foot-one and still growing, his best class was weight training, and, as was common with the Quinn brothers, he had a harem of girls who followed him everywhere.

Once Carter graduated and I was left without my "shield," Aidan took up the mantle and his harem didn't like it, but I tried to keep my head down and ignore them as best I could. Easy to do for the most part since I was dancing more than going to classes my junior year.

"My lips are sealed." I tried for a goofy grin. "This isn't a problem that you can make your bitch, buddy. We're just going to have to let it all play out naturally."

Carter crossed his arms and studied me. "If you go, I'm gonna miss your eighteenth birthday."

"I'll be back a full week before my eighteenth birthday, it's you who'll still be gone more than likely."

"You're breakin' our deal, Cass."

I scowled at him, my stomach churning. "You broke it first by running off to war!"

"So, this is about getting back at me?"

"No!" I snapped, and then took a deep breath. "No, seriously, it's not. The deal was we would have a private wedding ceremony by the dead tree with Torbig the Troll as officiant *when* I turn eighteen, right? I'm not eighteen. So, as long as you're back at some point before I turn nineteen, I will view the deal is intact. Unless of course, you find your forever love and marry her instead. At that point, I will admit that my heart will unequivocally shatter into a million pieces..." I let my sentence trail, hoping my joke would lighten the mood.

Carter laughed. "Fuckin' nut."

I giggled. "Says the bolt."

This had been a private joke I'd started back before I knew exactly what nuts and bolts were. At the time, he'd laughed hysterically, then explained the sexual connotation I'd inadvertently voiced, but still, the joke had stuck and it had been our thing.

"You're coming back, right?" he pressed.

"Are *you*?"

"Yeah, Cass, I'm coming back."

I slipped my hands into my pockets. "Well, so am I."

He wrapped his arms around me and drew me close. I pulled my hands from my pockets and hugged him back. I loved him more than I would ever admit out loud, but that was a story for another day. For now, it was time to grow up and figure out how to live my life without my crutch. It was something my mother had urged me to do... figure out how to exist in a world without Carter Quinn, but I'd always brushed her off, thinking one day, I'd have him forever. That he'd see me for something other than his best friend. But when he'd been recruited for the Air Force and jumped at the chance to be a hero, I realized he'd never see me the way I saw him, so I knew I had to let him go.

4

"I'm coming to the airport," he said, his voice low with emotion.

I squeezed my eyes shut. "You better."

"I'll email you every day that I can and you better do the same."

I smiled and leaned back to look up at him. "Do *not* go get all emotional and shit on me."

"Don't use that fuckin' language. You're too pretty for it."

"You're a dork." I laughed and shoved at him. "FroYo and a movie? I'll buy."

"You're not payin', Cass, but yeah, FroYo and a movie's good."

"Do you want to climb back down the tree or use the front door like a regular person?"

We had a huge tree that happened to have a sturdy limb that was like a ladder directly to my room. Carter had snuck in on more than one occasion, mostly when I was mad at him and refused to answer his phone calls. I'd tease him because if he didn't talk to me at least once a day, he couldn't seem to function.

"I didn't know your parents would be gone," he countered.

I giggled. "Whatever. I personally think you prefer the tree. Of course, it's the middle of the day, so you ringing the doorbell would have been perfectly acceptable."

He grinned. "Keep it up, buddy, and there'll be no movie for you."

"Oooh, you scare me," I retorted as I grabbed my keys and followed him out the door.

* * *

One week later, I stood with my dad and Carter at the end of the security line, not quite ready to say my final goodbyes as I headed to my next adventure. Daddy was flying to Paris with me and checking everything out before flying home, and Carter had offered to drive us so my mom could say goodbye at home. She was a wreck, so had readily agreed to do her sobbing in private. My sisters on the other hand had a life outside of me and were happy to wave at Carter's truck as we were driving away.

I was consumed with the fact that Carter was leaving in two days for his tour with the Air Force, which meant we'd maybe have a day or two to email or Skype, but then nothing was guaranteed.

I had done a really great job of keeping my warring emotions at bay. I was excited to go to Paris. I mean, it was freakin' Paris after all, but I knew I'd miss my family. We were tight. Like Carter and his family, only we were sisters, so we fought a little dirtier, but we loved each other and our parents rocked.

But leaving Carter made me sick to my stomach. I didn't know where he was going or where he'd be stationed... neither did he. The not knowing was the worst and if anything happened to him, I'd be the eighth to know, unless one of his brothers called me before my parents did. I blinked back tears at the thought, saying a silent little prayer to keep him safe.

"You okay?" Carter asked.

I forced a smile and nodded. "Yep."

"I think this is where we leave you, Carter," my father said.

Carter nodded and shook his hand. "Have a safe trip, sir."

My dad smiled and nodded, and I lost it, throwing my arms around Carter's neck and sobbing against his chest. "Ohmigod, Carter, if you get yourself killed in some Middle Eastern country, I will hurt you."

He chuckled, hugging me tight. "I'm not so easy to kill, Cass. I'm going to be fine, okay?"

I leaned back and he cupped my face, wiping my tears away with his thumbs. "Please stay safe," I whispered.

"I will. A bolt must return to his nut after all."

I rolled my eyes and nodded. "I love you."

"Love you too, Cass." He leaned down and gave me a gentle kiss on the lips. Not a romantic one, just one that reminded me he was my best friend and he adored me.

Dad and I walked through the point of no return and as I was putting my shoes back on, Carter waved to me, and I know he waited until he couldn't see me anymore before leaving. Don't ask me how I knew. I just did.

TWO

Carter

I WATCHED MY girl walk with her father toward their gate, smiling as she blew me a final kiss and then disappeared from my sight. I stamped down the pain of losing her, reminding myself that I'd see her again in a year and I'd finally be able to tell her how I felt. I'd kept my adoration of her quiet because she was young, sheltered, and the epitome of a good girl. It wasn't as though I was a bad boy... far from it, but I didn't want to be the one to take her virginity before she was ready, especially since her father would kill me if I did.

I wanted the timing to be right... when we were ready to make a life together. I'd dated a few girls, screwed a few girls, too, but it didn't take long for me to realize there would never be anyone else for me. Cassidy Dennis was mine. She had been since she was six and she would be until she was ninety-six. She was my best friend and I would wait for her as long as she needed me to.

Arriving at my truck, I swore when I couldn't get the door open. I'd lovingly restored my 1971 Ford pickup with my own two hands, and the occasional passing of a wrench or something from Cassidy. I'd always considered the truck just as much hers as mine, considering we'd talked for hours while I worked on it, but I still had a few things I needed to fix, including a sticky lock.

It took me a few minutes, but I managed to get the door open, and climbed inside. I started the engine and forced my desolation away. Cassidy would call me tomorrow, I'd hear her voice, and I'd know she was safe. I wished I'd been the one to go with her, but it didn't surprise me that her dad had taken up that responsibility. Her family was close, and Mr. Dennis wasn't about to let his baby go out of the country without fully vetting where she'd be living, who she'd be living with, the faculty and school.

I sighed. Cassidy had been gone fifteen minutes and my heart was heavy. As I reached for my wallet to pay for airport parking, my hand caught the chain I'd slipped into my pocket. At the end hung a nut and bolt, threaded together. I smiled and pulled it out, looping it over my neck. I'd kept it hidden from Cassidy because I'd had one made for her as well. A far more feminine version, granted, but matching all the same. I'd sneaked it into her carryon as she checked two bags at the ticket desk and I couldn't wait to hear what she thought.

My heart lightened as I headed home. I could do this. One year would go by quickly and we'd be able to pick up where we left off. It was our way and I knew nothing would change that.

* * *

Cassidy

I stared out the plane window and forced myself not to sob as we took off. Dad was on the aisle seat and we'd been pleasantly surprised to find that no one was between us.

"You okay, honey?" Dad asked.

I grimaced and turned to face him. "Is it wrong to feel like my heart is breaking?"

"Not at all." He smiled. "I promise, you'll be fine."

"But will Carter?"

"He's made of tough stuff, Cass. He'll be fine too." He took my hand. "Just focus on this year and if you're meant to be, you'll be. I know those are just words to you, but when you get some distance, things will be clearer."

I nodded, although, I knew he'd never understand. He was cursed (he said blessed, but I personally think he just replaced the word to convince himself) with a house full of women and womanly emotions, which meant drama was prevalent. Most things for my sisters, Shannon and Mia, were emotional tens (on a scale from one to…) when it came to boys and life. I was far more even-keeled, but that also meant I didn't openly share my love of Carter with the world. I did to my mom, but Dad's eyes would glaze over and Mom said he was going to his happy place when my sisters started in on their emotional blackmail, so Dad didn't know about the extent of Carter.

I turned back to the window and as soon as we were cleared to use our electronic devices, I pulled my backpack onto my lap and unzipped the front flap. Tugging out my iPod, I found a little wrapped package with Carter's distinctive script scrawled on the front.

I ripped it open and forced myself not to totally break down at thirty-five thousand feet. I pulled out a feminine but very sturdy silver chain that had a threaded nut and bolt, a pair of ballet slippers, and a mini dog tag hanging from it. It had been wrapped in tissue paper with a note.

> *To my favorite nut, here's a few things to remember me by. Kick ass in Paris and remember I'm just a phone call away. Love you,*
> *Cass*
> *Love, the best bolt you'll ever know, Carter*

"What's that?" my dad asked.

"A little surprise from Carter." I handed the chain to him and he smiled before handing it back.

"Clever," he said.

"That he is." I secured it around my neck and found myself reaching for it several times during the flight. I couldn't wait to call him and tell him how much I loved it and him. I didn't care that I was leaving for a year. I wanted him and if I had to wait for him, I would. Now I just had to convince him I was the one for him. That would prove harder.

Still, I had a smile on my face as I drifted off to sleep, my hand over the charms that had settled over my heart. Appropriate.

Little did I know, my phone call to Carter the next day would be too short to tell him anything substantial and the last time I'd hear his voice until I returned to the States. In less than a year, my safe little world would be rocked to its core.

* * *

Eleven months later…

"Cassidy!" Pierre grinned and held his arms out to me as I walked into the practice room. "*Vous êtes magnifique!*"

I chuckled as I accepted the double cheek kiss and hugged him back. I dropped my bag on the floor and pulled out my toe shoes. "*Bonjour* Pierre."

"Well done," he exclaimed. "You might just be fluent by the time you leave."

"You never know."

I had been in Paris for about a week when I was introduced to Pierre Desrosier. Tall and lanky, albeit muscular, he had the perfect dancer's physique and with his sexy French accent, I couldn't help but be drawn to him. Almost from the start, he'd pursued me and I was flattered. What initially gave me pause was that he looked quite a bit like Carter. I couldn't imagine dating anyone who looked like the love of my life unless it *was* the love of my life.

That had all changed three months ago, however. I'd received an email from Carter telling me that he'd met someone, and it was pretty serious. It wrecked me. Totally.

Lately, however, I was beginning to wonder if I should find out if it would work with Pierre. Granted, I had less than a month before I returned home, but who knows? It could be fun and who didn't love a power couple? Especially, when they were portraying a couple in art and happened to love each other in real life.

I deserved to be happy and move on just like Carter had.

"We will work on the transitions today, *oui*?"

Pulled out of my melancholic thoughts, I nodded. "Oui."

When our time came to an end, Pierre hugged me tightly. "Beautiful, Cassidy. You were so uninhibited today. Finally. *Parfait*." He stroked my cheek. "Have dinner with me."

I smiled. "Why not?"

"Oui?"

"Oui, Pierre. *Dîner serait belle*."

"I'll collect you at seven."

"Perfect... um... parfait," I corrected, and Pierre chuckled, kissing me on the cheek.

I headed back to my dorm room and took a hot bath. We'd worked out hard today and my body was hurting, but it was my heart that was suffering more. The moment I'd said yes to Pierre, I knew I had to let Carter go. Irrational, perhaps, but I didn't know if I could continue to hold out hope that he would ever be mine and it was time for me to live a little. I hoped it was, anyway.

After taking extra care with my hair and make-up, I opened the door to the handsome and incomparable dancer and let fate take my life wherever it led me.

* * *

One month later…

It was the beginning of October, and I had been home from Paris for just over a week and couldn't get out of bed. For the most part, my mother had left me alone to my depression up until now, but the morning before Carter was due home, she pushed into my room and sat on my bed. The time had come to confess.

"Okay, my sweet baby girl, I have given you some space, but now I'm really worried. I realize I have barely a week before you're eighteen and then I can't technically make you go to a doctor, but will you please tell me what's going on? Carter's coming home tomorrow, and I need to know why you're not excited. I need my Sassidy back."

"I'm not feeling very sassy today, Mom."

"What's going on, honey?"

"I did something. Something bad," I whispered.

She slid my hair away from my face. "Cassidy, what could you have possibly done that would make you dread seeing the man you love?"

"Mom, Carter's with someone else, please don't make it worse."

She sighed. "Which is all very weird."

"He's moved on. I did, too."

"What? What did you do?"

I sat up and pulled the covers up to my chest. "I can't tell you."

"Why not?"

"You'll hate me."

"Baby girl, there is nothing in this world that you could do that will make me stop loving you."

I tried to calm my churning stomach. "I slept with someone in Paris."

My mom took a deep breath. "Okay, honey. It happens. Was it someone you loved?"

"Not really, no." I shook my head.

"Was it Pierre?"

I nodded. "How did you know?"

"Well, he's handsome and you'd been spending a lot of time together," she said. "Plus, he looks a bit like Carter and I wondered if you'd be able to resist Carter with a French accent. I know I couldn't."

I snorted. "Well, I should have because I'm pretty sure I slept with him for all the wrong reasons."

"Oh, honey, been there." My mom smiled sympathetically. "Why do you think you slept with him?"

"I was mad."

"At Carter?"

I groaned with a nod. "Pierre was in the right place at the right time, I guess. Plus, I just thought I'd get it over and done with...the losing my virginity thing." I swallowed down the bile threatening to spill and dropped my face into my hands. "But I regretted it the second it was over."

"What happened?" Mom pressed.

"It was awful, Mom. I mean, sex wasn't as bad as I thought it would be... it didn't really hurt, but when I was naked with him he pointed out everything wrong with my body, and—"

"Like what?" Mom asked, her voice had taken on a weird shrill quality about it.

"My body?"

"Yes."

"Um, I have a large butt, my thighs are a little thick and

14

my breasts were bordering on porn sized."

"That little fucker."

"Mom!" I nearly choked, I was so surprised by my mother's swearing. It's not like she'd never sworn before, but I don't know that I'd ever heard her use the F-word.

"Well, he is. You're beautiful, Cassidy. Inside and out, and if that little shit couldn't see it, then good riddance."

"You're supposed to say that, you're my mom."

"I don't have to say anything of the sort."

"Mom," I groaned.

"You didn't sleep with him again did you?"

"No, but not because of what he said. I didn't know we weren't being exclusive. Apparently, I was one in a line of many. I am just such an idiot."

"Honey, we all make mistakes, and it's your time to make choices that push the limits. You can't be so hard on yourself."

I burst into tears. "No, you don't understand."

She gave me a gentle smile. "Tell me."

"I think I might be pregnant."

Mom gasped and wrapped her arms around me, pulling me close. "Oh, baby girl. Do you know for sure?"

I shook my head. "No, but I haven't gotten my period, and I'm sick all the time."

She stroked my hair. "When did you sleep with Pierre?"

"Right after the showcase."

"Which is when you were finishing those antibiotics for your strep."

I nodded. "Is that important?"

"They can make the pill useless."

I groaned. "But we used a condom."

"Which aren't a hundred percent," she said. "Look, let's not panic just yet. I'm going to run to the store and grab a test and we can know for sure."

"Thanks, Mom."

She smiled and left me, returning thirty minutes later.

"Go pee and we'll see what it says."

I nodded and took the box from her, grateful we were alone at least for the moment. I did my thing, washed my hands and then met my mom back in my room. For a few minutes, I felt like this could all be a cruel joke, but then there were two lines and my world crashed down again. I flopped onto my bed. "How am I going to tell Carter? He's going to hate me."

"I don't think he'll hate you, honey. I don't think he's going to be happy, but he won't hate you." She wiped away tears and shook her head. "Your dad on the other hand..."

"Ohmigod, Mom, we can't tell Dad."

"Well, how long were you expecting to keep it from him?" she challenged.

"I can't have Carter *and* Daddy hating me."

"Baby girl, neither of them will hate you. Daddy's going to freak out, I won't candy coat that, but he won't hate you."

"I'm a total whore."

"Honey, you are not a whore."

"Why are you so calm?" My mom was taking this news way too well.

My mom sighed. "Sometimes you do everything you're supposed to do, and shit just happens. Would I have wanted this for you? No. But it's happening and now we need to decide where to go from here. This could have happened to me before I married your father, so I'm the last person to judge you, honey. You just got stuck with some consequences I didn't."

"What does that mean?"

"Well, I wasn't always "safe" so to speak. I had a scare when I'd missed two pill days and had sex with my boyfriend at the time without condoms, so we've all been there, honey." She patted my knee. "We'll figure this out, Cass. It's not going to be pretty, but we'll figure it out."

"I can't tell Carter, Mom. He's only home for a week."

"Well, that's up to you, honey. But we need to tell your dad... and then your sisters."

I knew she was right, but that didn't mean I wanted to do it. In the end, we told my dad later that night and he said nothing. Not a word. Just stood and walked into his bedroom, closing the door behind him. Mom followed, and I was left to my thoughts, which turned me into a sobbing mess and kept me awake all night.

If I lost the love of my father, I'd be destroyed.

* * *

"Cass?" Carter called, jogging up to me. He was shirtless and delicious, his matching nut and bolt chain hanging against his pecs. He had a new tattoo on his upper arm of the Air Force logo and it was hot. He was leaving again in two days and I was silently congratulating myself for keeping my secret. He would go back to base and I could deal with my predicament in seven months, give or take.

"Hey," I said. We were out at the pond, cooling off on a particularly hot June day. I was sitting under the shade of the canopy his parents' had set up years ago, avoiding the sun.

He flopped down beside me and grinned. "So, you gonna fill me in?"

"On?" I asked.

"Why you've been so quiet these past few days."

I faced him, grateful my sunglasses hid my panic.

Um, you come home alone, you say nothing about the email you sent that broke my heart, and I'm pregnant with some asshat's baby. Of course, I kept that to myself and instead played dumb. "Have I been?"

"Cass, I know we haven't seen each other in a year, but I still know you."

"Just missed you."

"I've missed you too," he said, standing and holding his hand out to me. "Let's go for a walk."

"Mysterious." I took his hand and let him pull me up.

17

"Where are we going?"

We started toward the tree-line of our properties. "It's a surprise."

I giggled. "I love surprises."

"I know." He squeezed my hand. "I actually want to ask you something."

"Ask away."

"You know I love you—"

"I love you too," I said.

"No, wait. Let me get this out." He sighed. "Sorry. I'm fuckin' this up."

"You're doing fine."

"I love you, Cassidy. I have forever, and I want to know if you'll marry me when I'm done with this next tour."

I felt the color drain from my face. "What?"

He grinned as we arrived at the dead tree. "I have it on good authority Torbig the Troll will be available to do the honors when I get home... he told me himself... but I think maybe we should do the church thing."

"Wait. Carter." I knew tears were escaping the safety of my sunglasses, but I couldn't stop them.

"Hey, babe, why are you crying?" he asked, cupping my cheeks.

"I can't... ohmigod, Carter... I can't do this."

"Why not?"

"Ohmigod." I made an awkward attempt to walk away.

Carter grabbed my arm and pulled me to face him. "Hey, what's wrong? You can tell me."

I shook my head. "I can't tell you this, Carter."

He gave me a gentle smile. "I love you, Cass. You *can* tell me."

"You'll hate me."

"I could never hate you."

I flailed my hands at my sides in frustration. "Why didn't you tell me before I left how you felt?"

Carter frowned. "Because I wanted to wait until you were eighteen."

"What about your 'serious' relationship?"

"What serious relationship?"

Ohmigod, he broke up with her? And now he's telling me he loves me? No. I can't.

"Forget it. Just ignore me." I squeezed my eyes shut. "I need to go."

"Fuck me, Cassidy. What the hell is going on?" he snapped.

"I slept with someone. In France."

"O... kay," he said slowly. "Are you still together?"

I shook my head.

"Well, then, what's the problem?"

I laid my hands over my belly. "I'm pregnant."

"What?" he whispered, chuckling as though he didn't really hear what he heard.

"I'm pregnant. I made a stupid mistake and now I will be paying for that mistake for the rest of my life."

Carter's hands dropped to his sides and his face changed. I don't think I will ever forget the expression, mostly because I'd never seen it before... not from him, anyway. It was one of pure unadulterated devastation... one of disappointment and sadness... and, yes, a little hatred.

"I'm so sorry, Carter." I turned and made a run for my house. That was the last day I saw him. The last day I talked to him. The last day I spoke his name. After giving birth to Maverick and realizing that if I didn't get out of my tiny little farm town in Oregon, and away from the people who loved Carter Quinn, I would never escape him, so I moved. Not so far that I couldn't drive to my parents', but far enough that his name would never come up.

I had a beautiful little boy to think about and he would never know that his mother's heart had shattered irrevocably. He was my heart now and he was enough.

19

THREE

Ace

Four years later...

I PULLED MY bike up to the Quinn beach house and slid the kickstand down. I hadn't seen my family since I left, and as much as I missed them, I wasn't particularly sure I was ready for the barrage of questions I would inevitably have to endure.

But I'd promised. It was the fourth of July, after all, and the beach was a tradition.

"Uncle Carter!"

I looked up, unused to being called anything other than "Ace." I forced a smile as Jeremy, my nephew, rushed toward me. My eldest brother, Josh, had been married for over eight years now and had three kids. The rest of the Quinn brothers were still single and happy to be.

"Hey, bud. God, are you like twenty now?"

Jeremy laughed, hugging me and releasing me quickly. "Seven… but I'm totally a stud."

I ruffled his hair. "Said like a true Quinn."

"Are you and Uncle Aidan really in a motorcycle club now?"

"Yeah, bud, we are."

I had just become a full patched member of my club, which meant (for me, anyway) I had more freedom and money to do what I liked. I'd been a prospect for three years, having needed an outlet between tours, then as the tours became shorter, but the missions became more intense, it was my saving grace. A few of my "brothers" had been in similar situations and knew when to push and when to back off.

Aidan was still a prospect, and he'd probably become a full patched member eventually, but I didn't know when. Aidan always did what I did, even when we were kids, he was my constant shadow, so it was no surprise he followed me into the club, but he was young and still trying to find his place. He'd decided to become a vet, and since he was a huge horse fanatic, he'd been training and riding horses for a few years now, and I wondered if that would trump his desire to become a full-patched member. Time would tell, I guess.

I could fix, drive, and fly pretty much anything, which meant I was guaranteed employment in any one of the club's businesses, and now that I was a patched member, I was let in on every part of the businesses… legal or not so legal.

"Gram's been totally freaking out. I heard her tell Dad that if you crashed your bike, she'd hurt you."

"Well, we better get inside then." I grabbed my stuff and followed my nephew into the house.

"CarCar," my mother cried, and pulled me in for a hug. "You made it!"

She pulled away and patted me down as though to check

22

for injuries.

"Hi, Mom," I said, and smiled, kissing her cheek awkwardly. "I made it and I'm fine."

"It's bad enough Jaxon and Matt chose dangerous jobs, but now you and Aidan are riding motorcycles? I just don't know where I went wrong."

Still all about you, Mom, I thought in frustration.

"You didn't go wrong," I said. I disengaged from her as soon as I could, unable to stand even the briefest of embraces.

Her face fell, but she quickly recovered, plastering on a gentle smile and stepping back a little. "Your dad and brothers are on the deck."

I nodded and sidled around her, moving toward the back door.

"Thank you, honey."

I turned and smiled. "You're welcome, Mom."

She took a deep breath and made her way to the kitchen. I escaped her look of sadness and stepped onto the deck.

"Carter!"

My father's booming voice startled me for a second, but I recovered and smiled. "Hey, Dad."

Unlike my mother, my father gave me space. Perhaps a bit much, but no less appreciated. My uncle Ken had served in the Gulf war back in the nineties and returned changed which had affected my father deeply. They'd once been close, but he'd returned with PTSD, then ultimately died from the cancer that had stemmed from his time in the Middle East.

I never knew the details surrounding Ken's issues... I'd been too young, but my father had been apprehensive about me joining the military. Although, he'd been a little more open to me joining the Air Force. What they didn't know, was that I'd been recruited into the AFST, and trained as a para-rescue jumper, and had just completed my second mission... and it shook me.

Melanie, Josh's wife, walked toward me, smiling in greeting. "Hey, bud."

"Hey, Mel."

She gave me a quick hug and then headed into the house. My brothers walked toward me, almost in order of birth. Josh first, Matt second, Jaxon third (although he was fourth in the birth order), Luke next (third in birth order). All but Aidan and Jaxon hugged me, and just when I thought I'd lose my mind, they separated. I hated the close contact, but only Jax and Aidan knew the general extent of why.

The rest of the afternoon was spent in normal Quinn family conversation, food, and joking around, but it all seemed hollow to me. I felt disconnected. Even when we gathered on the sand for football, I moved through the exercise physically, but couldn't bring myself to enjoy it like I used to.

Just before midnight, after my parents, Josh and Melanie and their kids headed to bed, Jaxon and I sat on the deck, beers in hand, watching the ocean under the light of the moon. Luke and Aidan were in the garage playing a game of pool (our parents had converted the space five years ago when they realized the house wasn't going to accommodate the growing family) and we would sleep out there as well. Matt got a call, and being FBI, his off days weren't always guaranteed.

"You wanna talk about it?" Jaxon asked.

"No."

"You don't deal with shit, it festers."

"Thanks, Dr. Phil."

Jaxon smiled. "First kill?"

"No."

"Somethin' else first, though."

"Just leave it, Jax," I ground out.

"Gonna eat you up, Carter," Jaxon said.

I rose to my feet. "I'm goin' to bed."

"You're on the bottom."

"Fuck you, I'm not."

"Fuck you, you are," Jaxon corrected.

"We'll see."

I made my way into the house, ignoring Jaxon's laugh as I brushed my teeth and walked into the room that had been designated as ours for the trip. Not much had changed. It still had two sets of bunks, Jeremy and his brother, Carl, in one, which left the other for Jax and me. Our niece was in with Josh and Melanie, but I figured we would need to either get a bigger house or expand this one or we'd run out of creative sleeping options.

Too tired to deal with Jax and my play for the top bunk, I fell into the bottom one, hoping the sleeping meds would work tonight... I'd doubled the dose.

* * *

The setting sun cast shadows over my unit as our team lead, Ducky, signaled us into position. Gravel crunched under my feet as I eased forward, rifle raised. The shadows before me morphed into the form of a person. The barrel of an assault rifle pointed in my direction. My heart raced. Now or never. I ducked low, aimed, and fired. The scream of a woman pierced the silence. Bile rose in my throat and I rushed forward to see who I'd hit, expecting to see a stranger. A familiar face stared back at me, however, the accusation in her eyes turning my legs to jelly.

"Carter?" Cassidy let out a tortured groan as she grasped her bloodied chest and fell to the ground. "Carter!"

I bellowed in agony as pain sliced through my leg, and my eyes flew open to find my mother looking over me, tears running down her face.

"Fuck," I rasped, and tried to sit up.

"Honey? Are you okay?"

"Mom, back up a bit," Jaxon ordered, and gently pulled

her away.

"Boys, come here," Josh called, and I grimaced to see my nephews rush past me, obviously frightened by my display.

I folded my body out from under the bunk and dropped my face into my hands. "I'm gonna go."

"No, honey, please don't," my mother begged.

"Mom, I can't be scarin' the kids with this shit."

"We can sleep in the garage for the next few days," Jaxon countered. "Aidan and Luke can bunk in here."

"Please, Carter." She wrung her hands and I knew she wanted to hug me. "Let us help."

"No one can fuckin' help, Mom."

"Watch your tone, son," my father warned.

"It's okay, Scott."

"It's never okay to talk to you that way, Sheila."

"Sorry, Mom," I said. "I think it would be best if I go."

"No," she rushed to say. "Look, I get that this is hard, but you can't get on your motorcycle at three o'clock in the morning when you've had next to no sleep. Can you give it until tomorrow and if you still feel like you need to go, then we'll respect your wishes?"

I dragged my hands down my face. "I'm gonna go for a run."

"At this hour?"

"I'll go with," Jaxon said.

"Does that mean you'll stay?" she asked hopefully.

"For now," I said, and she relaxed.

I'd stayed until the following afternoon. Then I'd left and hadn't been back.

FOUR

Cassidy

Present Day...

"HEY, CASS," DANI said as soon as I answered the phone.

"Well, hi there, teacher of the year," I responded.

Danielle Carver had been Maverick's kindergarten teacher this past year, and she and I had begun a quick friendship which was one of the first I'd formed since leaving home. For whatever reason, I trusted Dani immediately. Rare for me, but Dani had championed Maverick, including spending extra time with him to help challenge him with harder work. Dani's husband, Booker, was an officer in the Dogs of Fire Motorcycle Club out of Portland, and not only was he gorgeous, he was wholly devoted to Dani and I was hoping I'd meet someone like him one day.

Dani giggled. "It's easy to look good when my kids are perfect."

I smiled at Mav who was drawing at the kitchen table. "Mine's pretty close... at least right now."

"Are you guys going to make it tonight?"

"Are you sure it's okay if I bring him?"

"Absolutely. Lily will be there, as will a bunch of other kids. Every member will be there tonight, so they picked up the biggest pig I've ever seen."

I lowered my voice. "So, you're telling me there will be more hotties like Booker and Hawk?"

Dani giggled. "Yes. Absolutely."

I grinned. "Then I'm definitely there."

"Awesome. Do you want Hawk and Payton to pick you up? They live in Felida and Payton offered."

"No, that's okay. I'm fine with driving. It means I can leave if Mav's tired."

"Sounds good. I'll send you Payton's cell in case you change your mind," Dani said. "Tonight's going to be really fun, Cass. I promise."

"I'm surprisingly looking forward to it... even with this sudden intense desire to back out."

Dani chuckled. "There is absolutely no pressure. We won't leave your side if you don't want us to. Austin and Hawk will run interference too."

"Thanks." I relaxed a bit, not realizing until then that I'd been nervous. "It's been a really long time, you know?"

"Well, it's time to get back on the horse then."

"Ha!" I retorted.

"I'll see you in a few hours."

I smiled. "Sounds good. 'Bye."

"'Bye," Dani said, and hung up.

I glanced around my little apartment and shook my head. How different my life was compared to how I had envisioned once upon a time. I had a really good job with a large insurance company, which afforded Maverick and me the ability to rent a clean but small two-bedroom apartment in Vancouver, Washington. We were finally starting to break through the years of struggle when I wouldn't have made it without my parents' help.

Once my dad had come to terms with my pregnancy, he became the best grandfather on the planet. Carter had left the day after I'd told him and I never heard from him again. If my parents heard any updates, they kept them from me, knowing I would have been unable to deal.

An unexpected friendship with Carter's older brother, Jaxon, had been a surprise, and he was actually the one who helped me get settled in Vancouver. He was an FBI agent and lived in Portland, so was close if I needed him. I rarely did and he kept his distance, but he'd check in every now and then.

I had lost all contact with Aidan around the same time as Carter left and I have no idea if either of them knew where I was or if they even cared. I guess for now, my sadness was replaced most days with a sort of fog that at least meant I wasn't overwhelmed with thoughts of what could have been.

"Mav, baby, we're going to a party tonight, so let's get you showered."

"Aw, Mom, do I have to?" he whined.

"Yeah, buddy, you have to. I don't want people thinking I don't know how to keep you clean and fed."

"Can I just tell them I'm a homeless kid you found on the street?"

I nearly choked on my intake of breath. Sometimes, he'd come out with these one-liners that were far too funny and mature for a six-year-old. "Holy moly, kiddo, you need to warn Mom when you're going to make me laugh like that."

He smiled. "Does that mean I can skip the shower?"

"Nice try, but no."

He grumbled again.

"Miss Harris, I mean, Mrs. Carver will be there, so you want to look your best, right?"

His face brightened. "Yeah! She's awesome."

"I know. I'll shower first, then you can while I put on my face."

Maverick wrinkled his nose. "Your face is already on."

I giggled. "It's a figure of speech."

He shrugged and went back to his drawing. He loved art. He always had. I suppose I shouldn't have been surprised, considering I'm technically artistic, but I was never able to draw like that... I didn't have the patience to sit in one place for long enough.

We arrived at the *Dogs of Fire* compound just after seven. I was very lucky to have a kid who was go-with-the-flow, considering I had more of a need for structure, but he was just happy all the time. I couldn't imagine my life without him, I just wished sometimes he could have been Carter's rather than Pierre's.

Dani met us at the front door and scooped Maverick into a big hug. "How's my favorite student? I'm gonna miss you next year."

"I'll visit, Mrs. Carver," he said.

"I can't wait. Do you want to come see what they're doing in the kids area? I think there's a video game battle happening."

"Can I, Mom?" he asked, his face bright with hope.

"Of course, bud. Let's go."

We made our way through the kitchen and to an area at the back with a huge kids' area and a couple of older teenage girls who were on babysitting duty. They seemed pretty solid and they were interacting with the kids, so I relaxed knowing Mav was in good hands.

"Ever since Payton and I forced our way in, there's always plenty of wine," Dani said as she pulled a bottle from the wine rack on the kitchen counter.

"Yeah, they've classed up the joint." An older woman

with a lot of makeup and teased bleach-blonde hair grinned. "I'm Susie. Prez's old lady."

I shook her hand and smiled. "I'm Cassidy. It's nice to meet you."

"You too, hon."

"What can we do to help?" Dani asked.

"Nothing. Pig's on the spit and we got more food comin', so we're good for now," Susie said. "I'll let you know when we're ready to eat. You can help then."

"Sounds good." Dani handed me a glass of wine and led me back into a large common room quickly filling with people. The space was chock full of sofas, overstuffed chairs, a pool table, large flat-screen television, several smaller tables that older kids gathered around for board games, and three outdoor picnic tables.

"There you are. I've been lookin' everywhere for you," Booker said, and leaned down to kiss Dani.

She giggled, breaking the kiss and slipping her hand into his back pocket. "Liar. You knew exactly where I was the entire time. You remember Cassidy, right?"

Austin "Booker" Carver took his eyes off his wife for a few seconds to smile and give me a chin lift. "Hey, Cassidy."

"Hi, Booker. Good to see you again."

We stood and chatted for a little while, pausing to greet Payton and Hawk who arrived half an hour later. Lily was excited to get back and see her friends, so we took her back and she fell right in with Maverick. I had a moment of intense pain when I watched them, heads together, as Maverick showed her how to use one of the video game controllers. This was about the same time I met Carter and, cockroach aside, he was just as patient with me as Mav was with Lily.

I laid my hand on my stomach and took a few calming breaths, before putting a bright, if not somewhat forced, smile on my face and followed Payton back out to the common room. I wondered if I'd ever stop loving him.

When nature called, I headed to the bathroom and once I was done, I washed my hands and pulled open the door. I nearly ran into a couple making out heavily in the hallway, and couldn't stop a tiny gasp as I steadied myself. "Sorry. Excuse me."

"No problem, babe," a deep voice said, but when the man turned to look at me, all time stood still.

I swallowed as I looked into the face of one Carter Michael Quinn. His hand up some woman's shirt, hers was down his pants, but they righted themselves as I gawked at them.

His face still just as gorgeous as I remembered, but his hair was quite a bit longer, some of it falling over his forehead as he shook his head. He wore dark jeans that sat low on his hips, motorcycle boots with buckles on the side, and a tight long-sleeved, black tee, with a leather vest over the top. The back of the vest proudly displayed the *Dogs of Fire* logo. He was just as tall as he'd always been, but he was now much, much wider. He'd obviously spent a great deal of the last few years working out, and his arms were bigger than my head, so it was apparently working.

He jumped away from the woman as though he'd just been caught cheating and his face contorted into rage. "What the *fuck* are you doing here?" he bellowed.

I was so shocked by the force with which he was speaking to me, I burst into tears. He had never raised his voice at me, not even when he was mad, and to have him yell at me so angrily was a total shock to the system.

"I...I...have to go," I hiccupped, and turned to make a run for it. I didn't even get one step away before I was dragged to face him again.

"I asked you a fuckin' question, Cassidy. What the *fuck* are you doing here?"

"Ace, baby." The woman we'd both seemed to have forgotten about pushed away from the wall.

"Take a hike, Lisa," Carter said, his eyes never leaving me.

"But..."

"Babe, fuck off."

I drew in a deep breath and bit my lip. He had never spoken to anyone like that before, and to see her expression go from disappointment to irritation, indicated to me that perhaps this was a first for her as well.

"Fuck you, Ace."

"Maybe later," he retorted, still staring at me, his beefy hand wrapped around my bicep.

She huffed and stomped down the hallway, leaving us to our reunion.

"Holy shit."

I turned to see Aidan Quinn walking towards us. "You're here too?"

He glanced at Carter and then back at me. "Where the hell have you been, Cass?"

"I...ah...around." I looked up at Carter again. "Can you let me go, please? I should leave."

"You're not goin' anywhere. What the fuck are you doin' here, Cass?" Carter repeated.

"I was invited."

"Cassidy?" Dani called as she rushed to join us. "Are you okay?"

"Get your fuckin' hands off her, Ace," Booker warned.

"Stay the fuck out of this, Book." Carter still continued to stare at me. "Answer the question, Cassidy."

"You know him?" Dani asked.

I nodded. "I used to."

"Fuck!" Carter bellowed.

Aidan just laughed.

"I should go home," I said again.

"No fuckin' way," he ground out. "You're comin' with me."

Booker stepped closer. "Ace."

33

"I swear to fuckin' *Christ*, Booker, you interfere, and you and I are gonna have a problem."

"Then you'll have a problem with me too, Ace," Hawk said as he made his way towards us, Payton following her face showing concern.

"Are you fuckin' shittin' me?" Carter bellowed again.

"Can you please stop yelling, Carter?" I whispered, still trying to bring my emotions under control. "You're giving me a headache, not to mention scaring the hell out of me."

"Nobody calls me Carter anymore, Cassidy," he said in warning.

"Not even your parents?" I challenged. "Or have you wiped them from your lives, too?"

"Fuck!"

I yanked my arm from his grasp and shoved at his chest. "Stop posturing, Cart... Ace, whatever you want to be called now. When did you become such a bully? If your mom heard you right now, she'd smack you upside the head!" My tears quickly dried up, although, the hiccupping continued until I took a few calming breaths.

I heard male chuckling behind me, but I didn't look... mostly because I couldn't stop staring at Carter. Good lord, the man could still render me immobile and, even though he was yelling and swearing more than I'd ever heard him, I knew he'd never hurt me. And damn it if seeing him in person didn't drive home how much I really still loved him.

He ran his hands through his hair then dragged them down his face. "You should go."

"Okay," I whispered, and started to head down the hall to get Maverick. Again, I didn't get far.

"Wait," Payton said. "I don't know what's going on, but you can't just chase her out."

"Babe," Hawk warned.

"What, Alex? Cassidy has as much right to be here as Ace. If he's so hell-bent on not seeing her, then perhaps he should leave."

"Actually, Ace has more of a right to be here, it being his club and all," Hawk countered.

"*Hawk*," Payton warned.

"It's fine, Payton. I'll just grab Maverick and go," I said.

"Maverick?" Carter said. "You named your kid Maverick?"

I nodded.

"Fuck me, Cassidy. Way to drive the knife in deeper." He scowled at me. "I'm fuckin' leavin'. Stay or fuckin' go. I don't give a fuck."

He stormed down the hall and out of my sight and I found myself sliding down the wall onto my butt in a puddle of tears.

Dani hunkered down beside me and squeezed my knee. "How about we take this somewhere private?"

"Take her to our room, babe," Booker said. "I'll text you when it's time to eat."

"Wait," Aidan said as Dani and Payton helped me up.

"You gonna give her trouble, Knight?" Hawk asked.

"Fuck you, Hawk," he snapped.

"It's okay," I said. "Can you guys give us a minute, please?"

They backed up a bit, giving me and Aidan a little privacy.

"Hey," he said, leaning against the wall and sliding down just enough so he could be eye level with me.

"God, Aidan, how tall are you now?" I asked.

"Six, six," he said.

I took a deep breath. "You always did have those big puppy hands and feet."

He smiled and cocked his head. "Are you doin' okay, Cass?"

"I'm fine. Good... yeah, good." I swallowed and forced myself to look at him. He was almost as gorgeous as Carter... almost. "How are you?"

Aidan crossed his arms and continued to study me. "I'm

good, Cass."

"How's Carter?" I rasped. A darkness covered his face and I shook my head. "You don't have to tell me, it's okay."

"He's different, babe. But that's not entirely your fault," Aidan said.

"Right." I folded my lips between my teeth and blinked back tears. "I'm sorry, Aidan."

"You got nothin' to apologize to me about, Cassidy. I love you like a sister, always have, always will. I had Ace's back because he's my brother, but that didn't change how I felt about you."

I gave him a sad smile. "Well, that's sweet, Aidan. Thank you."

"I don't do sweet, Cassidy."

I let out a quiet snort. "Oh, you absolutely do sweet."

He grinned. "We'll keep that between us."

I nodded, crossing my arms just to have something to do with my hands.

Aidan stood to his normal height again and I craned my neck to look up at him. "He'll come around."

"I just want him to be okay," I admitted.

"He will be." Aidan kissed my forehead, gave me a hug, and then led me back to Dani and Payton.

We headed upstairs to where the private bedrooms were. Dani unlocked a door and led us inside, flipping on the light and closing us in. "Make yourself comfortable, Cass. I'll grab some water."

I flopped into an easy chair by the window and Payton handed me a box of tissues before sitting in the chair beside me. I gave her what I'm sure was a pathetic smile and set the Kleenex on my lap. As Dani pulled waters out of a mini fridge in the corner, I took in the room. It looked like a pretty normal master bedroom, with a king-sized bed and a sitting area with television. I wondered how often they stayed here considering they had an amazing apartment overlooking the Willamette in downtown Portland.

"So you know Ace and Knight," Dani said, and handed me a bottle of water.

I nodded. "Since I was six."

"Wow," Payton whispered.

"Carter...um, Ace, was my best friend until... well, until I got pregnant."

"Is he Maverick's father?" Dani asked.

I shook my head and groaned as the tears flowed again. "Do you know how long it's been since I cried? Gah!"

"Well, you're obviously due," Payton observed.

As I pulled another tissue from the box, I filled these two virtual strangers in on everything. My life before Maverick and after, leaving no detail out. It was surprisingly cathartic, but it left me drained.

"Do you still dance?" Payton asked.

"When I can, but mostly in my living room nowadays."

Dani smiled. "Why was Ace so upset about you naming Maverick, Maverick?"

"Because in my heart, he's Carter's. Carter always had this weird obsession with flying, and could probably quote *Top Gun* beginning to end. He made me watch it more than a dozen times, until I said no more." I grimaced. "It was a given that he'd go into the Air Force, and when I was in the hospital giving birth to this beautiful little boy, all I could think about was how he should have been his, you know?"

"He kind of looks like him," Dani said. "Sorry."

I sighed. "Don't be. He does look like him, but that's not a surprise. Pierre looked a lot like Carter at the time. It's probably why I let him manipulate me." I groaned again. "I don't understand what Carter's even doing here! Last I heard he was in the Middle East somewhere."

"I think he's been part of the club for a while," Dani said. "But I don't know for sure. He does different stuff than Austin and Hawk."

Payton grimaced.

"What?" Dani asked.

Payton shook her head. "Nothing."

"No, if it's about Carter, tell me," I said.

"He's got a reputation," Payton said. "Like a bad reputation. He sleeps with a different woman every night, rarely repeats... Lisa's the only one he's kind of kept around, but they're not exclusive or anything. Plus, he likes to fight."

"Women?" I asked, horrified.

"No!" Payton rushed to say. "Well, at least, I don't think so. Alex said he'd never hurt a woman, but he warned me to stay away from him because of... well, Alex gets jealous. He gave me the same speech about Mack, but for different reasons. Mack's a lover and sleeps around because he's charming and sweet and women thank him, even when he's showing them the door. Mack doesn't have an enemy on the planet... Ace, not so much. He's kind of a dawg and doesn't care who he hurts."

I groaned. "Great."

"Sorry, Cass," Payton grumbled.

"I should probably get out of here before he comes back."

"I think you should stay," Payton countered. "At least until you feel okay to drive. Eat something and get a little energy back in your body."

"I *am* kind of hungry."

Payton smiled. "Well, it's a good thing you're here then. There's always more than enough food."

"Thanks for being so... I don't know... un-chick-like. Ever since I moved up here, I don't get to see my sisters much and I miss them."

Dani waved a hand dismissively. "It's not a problem. We'll grow your girl mob, just wait and see. Kim will be here later and she's a hoot."

"Your best friend?" I asked. Dani had talked a little bit about her best friend's exploits over the last year, so I had an idea of who she was.

"One in the same."

I smiled. "Sounds fun."

Payton pulled her phone from her pocket and glanced at the screen. "Food's up. Hawk's got the kids."

"Is there somewhere I can freshen up?" I asked.

"Yeah. Use my bathroom," Dani offered.

I rose to my feet and headed through the door Dani pointed to.

FIVE

Ace

I PULLED UP to my brother's house and slid my kickstand down. I allowed my emotion to take hold again as I dragged my helmet off. I'd buried my rage, unwilling to risk myself or my Harley on the drive over. But Cassidy fuckin' Dennis. Shit.

She'd always been rail thin and muscular, the perfect ballerina, but now, she'd filled out. She had an ass I wanted to grab and tits I wanted to bury my face in. She was still just as gorgeous as I remembered, her blonde hair a mass of soft curls that I wanted to run my fingers through. She used to keep her hair at shoulder length, but now it was halfway down her back and it suited her. She'd worn dark jeans that hugged her heart-shaped ass, and a tight, long-sleeved T-shirt that showcased every gorgeous curve. Fuck!

I stomped up the stone steps and pounded on the door. Jaxon didn't answer right away, so I pounded again.

"What the fuck?" Jaxon snapped as he slammed the door open, his gun at his side. "Carter?"

I shoved my brother back and stepped inside. "Did you fuckin' know?"

"Did I fuckin' know what?"

"Don't fuck with me, Jax. Did you know where she was?"

My brother sighed and closed the door, locking it before sliding his gun into the holster he'd left on the kitchen counter. "Yeah. I knew where she was."

"Did Aidan?"

"No. I don't think so."

I slammed my helmet and gloves onto the sofa and scowled. "God *damn* it, Jax. Why the fuck didn't you tell me?"

"Because you asked me not to."

"And you figured that would be the one fuckin' request you'd listen to?"

"Beer?" Jaxon asked, pulling open the fridge.

"No." I paced the great room.

Jaxon shrugged, grabbing himself a bottle and flopping onto his recliner by the fireplace. "So, what happened?"

"She showed up at the club."

"Fuck. Seriously?"

"Where the hell has she been this whole time?" I demanded.

"Vancouver."

"Do Mom and Dad know?"

"No idea," Jaxon said, and sipped his beer. "I wouldn't be surprised if they did, but then again, I wouldn't be surprised if they didn't."

"Helpful, Jax, thanks."

"Sit down, Carter, you're making me dizzy."

I lowered myself onto the sofa and dropped my face into my hands.

"What are you going to do?"

"No fuckin' clue," I admitted.

"You don't have to see her again, right?"

I shook my head.

"But?" Jaxon pressed.

"But, how do I never see her again when I know where she is?" I glanced at my brother. "She named her kid Maverick."

"I know," Jaxon admitted.

"Fuck!"

"Look, she's a good girl, Carter. She made a mistake when she was seventeen and she lost you in the process, but she doesn't date, she doesn't do anything except take care of her son. You can't fuck that up unless you're willing to forgive her and move on."

"I have."

Jaxon raised an eyebrow in disbelief.

"What? She fuckin' shut me out!"

"You *left*, brother," Jaxon reminded him.

"She fucked some douchebag Frog and had his fuckin' baby! What choice did she leave me?"

"You act like she cheated on you, Carter."

"What would you call it, Jaxon?"

Jaxon shrugged. "She didn't know how you felt about her. And how many women did you fuck before her?"

"She knew about them!"

"And that makes it better? Any scares with a busted condom, Carter? Any time where you might have said, 'Fuck it, I'll go ungloved tonight'?"

"Fuck you, Jaxon."

42

"You're not my type." He drew in a sip of beer. "How 'bout you cut her some slack?"

I dropped my face in my hands again and squeezed my eyes shut. Jaxon was right. He was always right, but what I still wasn't ready to admit was that I was more to blame for Cassidy's mistake than anyone. If I'd just let her know how I'd felt, confirmed she felt the same way, then none of this would have happened. She may have still gone to Paris, but she sure as hell wouldn't have slept with someone else. Of that, I was certain.

"Better?" Jaxon asked.

"No." I sat up and settled my ankle over my knee. "I fucked up, Jax."

Jaxon took another swig of my beer and nodded. "You gonna fix it?"

"Don't think I can."

"Won't know unless you try."

I studied my brother. "She really doesn't date?"

"Yep."

"Do I want to know how you know that?"

"Nope."

"You're a pain in the ass, you know that right?" I retorted.

Jaxon grinned and nodded.

I grabbed my helmet and stood. "Well, as fun as this has been, I'm gonna get out of here."

Jaxon pushed out of his chair and followed me to the door. "I'll run by your place and grab the dog for the night… give you a chance to figure some shit out."

"Thanks."

"Love you, dumbass."

I chuckled. "Love you too, asshole."

I climbed on my bike and made my way back to the club. I hoped Cassidy was still there, because if she disappeared on me again, I might destroy something.

* * *

Cassidy

I was in the club kitchen wiping Maverick's face with a wet paper towel when I felt the temperature in the room change. I glanced up to find Carter walking toward me and my heart raced as he approached.

"Ow, Mom," Maverick whined.

"Oh, sorry, honey." I focused back on him and lifted his chin. "You're good to go play if you want."

He took off into the playroom and I made myself busy with washing dishes and loading the dishwashers. I hadn't been alone in the room, but within seconds I was...the rest of the women scurried out quickly and quietly.

"Cass," Carter said, and settled his hip against the counter next to me.

"Hmm-mm." I stepped to the side, not wanting to look at him.

"Don't do that."

"Do what?" I asked, scrubbing a plate a little harder than it needed.

"Shut me out." He laid his hand on top of mine and pushed the plate back in the sink. "Can we talk?"

Still not looking at him, I shook my head. "No."

"I guess I deserve that," he said.

"And a whole lot more," I mumbled. I noticed out of my peripheral that he crossed his arms which just made him appear even bigger than he was. Good lord, he must have put on a hundred pounds of muscle.

"Talked to Jaxon," he continued.

I paused in my scrubbing, a little taken aback by what he said. Had he not talked to Jaxon before? I set the plate in the dishwasher and went about scrubbing the next one.

"He filled me in on everything," Carter continued.

Scrub, load, scrub, load.

"He thinks it's all your fault."

"What?" I gasped and glared up at him. "He does?"

"No." Carter smiled. "I just wanted you to look at me."

"Jerk." I wrinkled my nose and stared back down at the sink.

Carter chuckled, and I don't really know what came over me, but the sprayer was *right there*, and he was also right there, and, well, he deserved it. A great sense of relief settled over me as he jumped away from the sink and let out a strangled expletive.

I smiled smugly and went back to the dishes. My mistake. I shouldn't have turned my back on the beast. Without warning, I was lifted and gently thrown over his shoulder, his hand landing with a smack on my bottom.

"Carter!" I squealed, only I couldn't quite get enough breath to say anymore.

I felt air move through my hair as he walked me across the common room and up the stairs. He put me down in front of a door and then unlocked and opened it, guiding me through. "We're gonna talk."

I crossed my arms and waited while he turned the light on and closed the door behind him. "I need to check on Maverick."

"Your son's fine, Cass. Payton will make sure."

"And how do you know that?"

"Because I just sent Hawk a text," he said, and dropped his phone on a nightstand next to a very large bed. He waved a hand toward the chairs at the end of the bed. "Have a seat, babe."

"I'm not your babe," I grumbled, but did sit down.

"Your family still call you 'Sassidy'?"

"What's that got do to with anything?" I snapped.

"Nothin', ba—I mean, Cass." He dragged the chair next to mine to settle in front of me, folding his humongous body into it and leaning forward. I studied my lap. Carter covered

45

my hands with his and squeezed gently. "Hey."

I met his eyes and forced back tears. "What?"

He grimaced. "We have a lot to talk about."

I shrugged and dropped my head again.

"Look at me." When I did, he smiled gently. "I'm sorry, Cassidy."

Those three words broke me. Shattered me into a million pieces and I found myself pulled onto his lap and sheltered in his embrace while I sobbed into his chest.

"Shhh, baby, it's okay," he whispered.

"Why didn't you marry her?" I asked.

"Who?"

"The woman you emailed me about."

"What woman I emailed you about? I didn't email you about any woman."

I shoved myself off his lap with a frustrated growl. "Yes, you did! You said you met someone and it was serious."

"Cass, I never sent you a fuckin' email. There was never any other woman. It has always been you. I should have told you how I felt," he said sadly. "If I had, you would have waited."

I dragged my hands down my cheeks in an effort to dry them. "What do you mean, you should have told me?" I asked with a sniffle. "How long did you feel that way? Was it before... you know?"

"Yeah." Carter sighed. "Remember Shelly?"

"Your senior year girlfriend... the one you took to prom?"

He nodded, pulling me back onto his lap. "I shouldn't have taken her to prom."

"What?" I frowned. "Why not?"

"Because I should have taken you."

"Ohmigod, Carter, don't be a dork." I pushed at his shoulder. "You were totally into her."

"No, I was totally into sex and she gave it up... a lot."

"Ew, okay, I didn't really need to know that," I ground

46

out.

"I thought I could deal with my feelings for you and still screw around. What I realized on prom night was that I loved you and there would never be anyone else."

I scrambled from his lap again. "What?"

He rose to his feet, but I held my hand out to keep some distance. He crossed his arms but didn't come any closer. "I had this misguided sense of something, I don't know what... bullshit really, that if I said out loud how I felt, I'd take your virginity before you were ready, and then I'd feel guilty because I knew I was leaving. I guess I just wanted you to have the freedom to get through high school without that weighing on you."

I shook my head. "You loved me back then?"

"Yeah, Cass. It's why Shelly was the last one... well, until..."

I blinked back tears again. "God! I am so sick of crying!"

"Sorry, babe."

"Still not your babe," I snapped. "Is that why you came over that night? You said Shelly had gotten sick and you drove her home."

"Kind of true... I broke up with her."

I gasped. "You dumped her on prom night?"

"Yeah." He had the good sense to look contrite.

"Wow, that's a dick move, Carter, especially for you."

"I thought you'd be happy!"

"You thought I'd be happy that you dumped a girl for me on prom night?" I asked. "A night that's supposed to be special, but not only did you break her heart, you then didn't feel the need to tell me you'd dumped a girl for me? Think about what you just said, buddy, and let me know if you still think I'd be happy."

"Fuck!"

"Shelly was *nice*!"

"But she wasn't *you*!" he snapped. "God damn it, Cassidy, why the fuck can't I win with you?"

"I didn't know this was a contest!"

He settled his hands on his head and scowled. "I think we need to take a minute."

"Why?" I challenged. "What is any of this supposed to accomplish?"

"I love you, you fuckin' nut!"

"You said you were moving on!"

"Never said I was moving on, Cassidy."

"You stopped all communication, Carter. If you loved me, you could have at least kept in touch. Let me know you were okay."

"And if you loved me, you wouldn't have fucked some French asshole and had his baby."

I hissed through my teeth, his barb a direct hit. "Well, you're right about that, I suppose."

"Oh, fuck, Cass," he rushed to say, "I'm sorry. I didn't mean it."

He headed toward me again, but I shook my head. "I think... I think I need to go."

"No, don't. God, Cass, just hash it out with me. I can't lose you again."

"And I can't have my past sins constantly shoved in my face!" I swallowed. "Not by you. I won't survive it."

Carter nodded, his face stricken with sadness. "You made a mistake, Cass. God knows I've made a shit ton myself... you just got stuck with—"

"If you say I got stuck with a consequence, I will end you. Maverick is not a consequence. He's the best thing that ever happened to me and if I had the chance to go back and change what I did, I wouldn't," I sobbed. "Because I got him and he's worth it." Again, with the fucking crying. Damn it! I needed to get hold of myself.

Carter wrapped his arms around me again. "I'm sorry, Cass. Seriously. I will never bring it up again."

"You can't make me choose between you and him, Carter. You'll lose."

He lifted my chin and cupped my face. "Does that mean I have a shot here?"

"That's not what I mean."

"Answer the question."

"Do you want a shot?" I challenged.

"Yeah, baby, I want a shot." He kissed me gently and then stroked my cheek. "I love you, Cassidy. That never stopped. I ran because I'm an asshole, but I figured out, kind of recently, that some... no, a lot... of this is on me."

I took a deep, shaky breath. I wasn't quite ready to let myself believe he was standing in front of me.

"Please, Cassidy," he whispered.

"I... I don't know."

"You take all the time you need, babe. I'm not going anywhere."

I pushed away from him and wiped my face again. "I don't know where we go from here, Carter. Our lives are so different now. I don't know how to make them mesh."

"We can figure it out as we go. There's no pressure."

I snorted. "There *is* pressure, Carter. I have a child to think about now."

"And I will get to know him."

I shook my head. "Not yet."

"What the fuck, Cass?"

"I need to know if this is going to work before you 'get to know him.'"

"It's going to work, babe, because I'm not losing you again."

I let out a groan of irritation. "So, that hasn't changed."

"What's that?"

"Your need to make every situation your bitch."

He chuckled. "There's nothing we can't accomplish together."

"Well, thank you, Maya Angelou." I flopped back onto the chair.

"Hey." He followed, sitting across from me again. "You

49

still love me?"

"No."

Carter smiled. "Liar."

I studied him for several seconds and then rolled my eyes. "Yes, I still love you, you dipshit bolt."

"Love you too, nut." He grinned as he reached into his shirt and pulled out a chain that was around his neck. Attached to it was the matching nut and bolt to mine and his dog tags. "I still haven't taken it off."

I bit my lip and pulled out mine. "Me neither."

He lifted my hands to his lips and kissed my palms. "I will do anything, Cassidy. Whatever you need me to do, but I won't lose you again."

"I don't know how to get past the hurt... the hurt I've caused you more than anything."

"I know. We'll have to figure it out, but if you promise to dig in with me, I'll do the same. I forgive you, baby. Do you forgive me?"

I nodded. "Yes."

"Are you going to figure this out with me?"

"Do I have a choice?"

He chuckled. "No."

I leaned forward and laid my head on his lap. "Can we wait to tell our families anything for a little while?"

"Yeah, baby, we can." He stroked my hair. "But I want to meet Maverick."

I nodded. "Fine."

"Why'd you call him Maverick?"

I sat up and smiled. "Why do you think?"

"Fuck me, Cassidy. I love you." He rose to his feet and pulled me with him, wrapping his arms around me.

"I'm thinking now wouldn't be a good time to tell you what his middle name is."

"Carter? Seriously?"

I blinked up at him. "I just said now would *not* be a good time to tell you that."

He chuckled. "You didn't say I couldn't guess."

"Not really the point, Carter."

"Kind of is the point, Cassidy." He cocked his head. "Backtracking a bit, what did you mean by you didn't know I was okay? I sent you letters."

"No you didn't."

"Babe, I *did*. We almost never had reliable internet, so I sent two handwritten letters in the packages I sent home with a note for my mom to forward to you. I had one or two opportunities to send stuff home, so I packaged shit up together. I know my brothers got everything I sent, so I'm sure she would have forwarded."

"Well, I didn't get anything from you, Carter, except that email, so I don't know what to tell you."

"I'll talk to my mom and figure it out, honey, but I swear to Christ I sent you letters."

I bit my lip and nodded. "Okay."

"How do you want to handle the Maverick thing?" He stroked my hair. "Me establishing myself in your lives?"

"I don't know. I guess we'll take it slow. He knows who you are... sort of."

"He does?"

I slipped out of his arms and nodded. "I have a couple of pictures of you that he's looked at more than a few times. I have the one of you in your flight suit and the one in your uniform, remember? You gave them to me after BMT? Plus, all the ones from when we were kids."

Carter nodded. "I didn't think you'd keep 'em."

"I have everything you ever gave me, Carter," I said. "Maverick obviously didn't see you walking toward the kitchen earlier or he probably would have called you by name. You have always been Uncle Carter in my home."

"Shit, Cass! *Uncle* Carter? I'm not your fuckin' brother!"

"Well, I'm sorry, Carter, what would you have had me tell him instead? 'Honey, this is Carter. He was my best friend a long time ago, and I still love him more than anyone

51

in the world outside of you, but I decided to screw your biological father and now the love of my life won't speak to me. Please bear with me while I never date another man as long as I live, and a part of my heart never truly heals, probably because I named you after him, all the while we'll stare at his pictures together and wish for what could never be'?" I sighed. "I think that would make me a pretty crappy mom, buddy. It was easier to just say you were Uncle Carter, and you were off flying planes and saving the world." I looked up at him and rolled my eyes. He was staring at me as though I had lost my mind. And then he let out a roar of laughter that had me scanning the room for something to throw at him. "Bite me, Carter Quinn!"

He continued to laugh, but picked me up and threw me gently on the bed where he covered my body with his and kissed me, his laughter and my irritation drying up pretty quickly. I had never been kissed like this. Don't get me wrong, I'd been kissed before, but even Pierre, who I considered to be a boyfriend regardless of how long it lasted, never kissed me like this. I knew Carter would be good at this... he was good at everything... but I hadn't banked on just how good. He slid his tongue into my mouth and I met it with mine, arching into him when he slid his hand under my shirt and cupped my breast. He tugged one of my bra cups down and ran a fingernail over my nipple, making it pebble instantly.

His mouth moved to my neck, his warm breath against my skin sending shivers down my spine. "Baby," he whispered. "God, Cass, you're amazing."

"Wait, Carter." I pushed at his shoulders.

"Huh-uh," he whispered against my skin. "Not waiting anymore."

"No, Carter. Stop." I pushed at him again.

He rolled off me. "What the hell?"

"I'm not doing this with you."

"Ever?"

I blushed. "Well, no, but certainly not today."

"Why?"

I slid off the bed. "Oh, I don't know... maybe because you had your hand up another woman's shirt less than three hours ago."

"Fuck!" he hissed.

"*And* you offered to do that to her later."

"Cass—"

"*And* you have a reputation of being a total man whore."

He sat up and scowled. "Who the fuck have you been talkin' to?"

"That's not important."

"Yeah, it fuckin' is, Cass. Those bitches—"

"Please don't call them bitches."

"Fuck me, Cassidy," he ground out. "If those women can't keep their mouths shut, don't matter that they're old ladies, we're gonna have a problem."

"Well, you better get over that really quickly, buddy, because I like them, and I honestly don't get the impression they're going around saying anything to anyone else. They were simply filling me in on what they'd heard from their *husbands*, mind you, so if you have an issue, talk to them." I crossed my arms. "Just don't start a fight."

"Holy shit, woman, what the fuck does that mean?"

"I just heard you like to fight, which surprised me a little, because you were always so good at keeping your anger in check."

"Yeah, well it's been a shitty few years, Cassidy, but that's not really the point—" Before he could finish whatever he thought would change my mind, his phone buzzed on the nightstand. He groaned and grabbed for it, letting out a frustrated sigh. "Maverick's looking for you."

I nodded, setting my clothes right. "I'm the worst mom ever."

"Baby, calm down. He's safe. We'll go down and check on him."

"I shouldn't have to get a text from another person telling me he's looking for me! I should be down there with him—" I ranted as I fixed my hair, "—not up here letting you paw at me."

"Paw at you?" Carter laughed. "I haven't even begun to paw at you."

"Carter, shush." I closed my eyes, my body thrumming with desire. I couldn't *wait* for him to paw at me for real.

"Cassidy Eleanor Dennis." I felt Carter's hand on my waist and looked up at him.

"What?" I whispered.

"You're a great mom. There isn't a person in the world who would argue that point. And I know Payton and Dani enough to know that they would make sure Maverick's safe and happy, regardless of if it's for a minute or a year, so that text was a courtesy text. Not a 'get down here right now' text. Hawk would have said something different if it was."

"You think so?"

"I know so. They may be loose with their opinion of me, but you, they love."

"I think they like you just fine, but yeah, they like me better, which is why I was warned."

"Figured." He smiled and leaned down to kiss me quickly. "Now, let's go find Maverick."

I nodded and followed him downstairs.

SIX

Cassidy

WE ARRIVED IN the common room to find Maverick playing pool with Hawk, Booker, and Lily. "Mom!" he called. "I'm winning."

"Wow, kiddo, that's awesome." I grinned and made my way to him. I cocked my head and asked Hawk and Booker, "You're not turning my kid into a shark, are you?"

Hawk chuckled, and Booker shrugged.

"I can't be a shark, Mom," Maverick said. "I'm a human, but did you know that sharks have to keep swimming or they die?"

"I think I heard that somewhere."

His eyes went to Carter, as though just noticing him, and they widened before tugging on my hand. I leaned down and he whispered in my ear (loudly), "That looks like Uncle

Carter."

"That's because it is." I smiled and straightened. "Maverick, meet Carter."

Carter hunkered down beside him, which was good, since he was four times the size of Mav. "Hey, buddy. Your mom's told me so much about you."

Maverick stuck his hand out and shook Carter's hand, just the way I'd taught him, and I had an immediate moment of pride in my son.

"I've seen your pictures and my middle name is Carter," Maverick said. "Are you really a pilot?"

"I was. I don't get to do it as much as I'd like to anymore, but yes, I still fly."

"That's okay," Maverick said. "Mom doesn't dance as much as she'd like to anymore, except when she's dancing with Kevin, but sometimes she dances in our living room. Maybe you could do that too."

I bit back a giggle at my son, the encourager, trying to help Carter find a way to do what he loved.

"It's your turn, Maverick," Lily said. Her little voice incredibly sweet and adorable. I wondered if I should talk to Payton about a marriage contract.

"Thanks, Lily," he said, and chalked his cue like a professional.

Carter stood close to me, his front touching my back as we watched Maverick try to maneuver a stick taller than him on a table he could barely reach.

"Who's Kevin?" he whispered.

"A friend."

"A dancer."

I smiled as Maverick set up his shot. "Yeah. We take a ballet class together a couple of times a month."

I felt Carter relax. "So, he's gay."

I snorted. "Not even close."

Carter's body locked again, but before he could say anything further we heard a feminine voice call, "Ace?"

He and I turned as one to see the woman he'd been making out with earlier standing next to one of the sofas.

"Yeah, Lis?" he said, his voice somewhat irritated.

"Can we talk?" she asked.

"Be nice," I whispered, and turned back to the pool game.

"Yeah," he said, and walked away.

* * *

Ace

I didn't want to talk to Lisa. I wanted to stay and watch the game with Cassidy, but I supposed I owed Lisa some kind of explanation.

Following her down the hall and into one of the meeting rooms, I closed the door behind us and leaned against it. "What's up?"

"What do you mean, 'what's up'?" she snapped. "You fucked me last night and we had plans today and you fuckin' blew me off."

I frowned. "We're not exclusive, Lisa."

"I know we're not exclusive, Ace, but I changed my plans to be here today, and you know it. You better fuckin' explain why you took off and left me without a word, and I swear to God, if it's about that tiny little bitch out there, you and I are gonna have a problem."

I saw red as I shoved Lisa gently but firmly up against the wall, my hand on her chest. "You ever fuckin' call her a bitch again, Lisa, you are gonna have a bigger fuckin' problem than me blowin' you off."

She scowled up at me. "Fuck you, Ace."

"No. Never again, Lis. Why don't you go ahead and fuck off?" I lowered my hand and walked out the door.

"You're a fuckin' asshole," Lisa yelled as I made my way back to Cassidy.

It was for me, but I refused to waste any more time... or

breath on the whore down the hall. I arrived in the common room to find Cassidy leaning over the pool table, her perfect little ass on display for everyone, and I felt irritation rear its head.

I noticed Train, one of the young recruits, eyeing her and headed to him immediately. "Look away, Train, or I will fuckin' remove your eyes from their sockets."

"Sorry, Ace," he grumbled, and walked toward the kitchen.

The recruit taken care of, I turned back to Cassidy, only to find Mack, one of my brothers, leaning over her showing her how to make a shot. Mack typically ran with Booker, but when he wasn't, he was usually somewhere with a woman… or two. Man-whore would have been a far softer description of the young attorney, and I didn't want him anywhere near my woman.

"Mack," I ground out.

"Ace." Mack grinned, but didn't look at me or remove himself from Cassidy. Instead, he ran his hand over her arm and repositioned it. "Like this, babe. It'll put less spin on the ball and you'll be able to get it in the pocket."

Cassidy pulled her arm back and shot the cue forward, the clack of the white ball hitting a solid, and then her little squeal of victory as the solid slid into the pocket. I went hard at the sound.

"Ohmigod, it worked," she said. "Thanks, Mack."

"Anytime, babe."

"Fuck off, Mack," I hissed.

"Carter!" Cassidy snapped. "Language."

"Yeah, *Carter*, there are kids around. What's your problem?" Mack glanced at me with a shit-eating grin on his face, still touching Cassidy.

I faced my brother, my back to the kids and mouthed "fuck off" again before inserting myself between Cassidy and Mack, shoving the man out of the way. Mack's response was to laugh, although, he did put distance between us.

I wrapped an arm possessively around Cassidy's waist and pulled her close, only to have her worm her way out of my hold and step closer to Maverick. She sent me a look that spoke volumes, though, and I frowned at her. I picked up that she didn't want public displays of affection around her son, at least not yet, but that didn't mean I had to like it.

I crossed my arms over my chest and watched as Hawk helped Lily make a shot, even though it was boys against girls. Lily stared up at her dad with hero worship in her eyes and I hoped I'd have that one day. I wanted nothing more than to have kids with Cassidy... I just had to figure out how to make it happen sooner than later.

A few minutes later, once the girls had "won" the game, Cassidy declared it was time to get Maverick home and into bed.

"Aw, Mom, Lily and I were going to play Super Smash Bros."

"I'm sure Mrs. James and I can figure out a time for you and Lily to have a play date. Maybe at our place," Cassidy countered. "So, you can play another day."

"But we don't have Super Smash Bros," Maverick whined.

"But *we* do," Payton interjected. "You can come over anytime and play."

"Can I, Mom?" he begged.

Cassidy nodded. "I will set something up with Mrs. James, okay?"

Maverick let out a fist pump and grinned. "Awesome!"

"Did you leave anything in the playroom?" Cassidy asked.

"Oh, my DS," he said.

"I'll help you find it," Lily offered, and the two made a run for the playroom.

I watched them go and then smiled down at Cassidy. "Brings back a few memories, huh?"

She nodded and turned away, but not before I caught the sheen of tears in her eyes. I slid my hand to her neck and gave her a gentle squeeze, kissing her temple.

"I guess we should exchange phone numbers," she murmured, and pulled her phone from her pocket, effectively pulling away from me.

I took her phone, entered my info, then texted myself. I was handing her phone back just as Maverick and Lily returned, portable gaming console in hand.

"Found it," Maverick declared.

"Good job." Cassidy took a few minutes to say her goodbyes and then I walked them to Cassidy's car.

"Get yourself buckled, Mav," she instructed. "I'm going to talk to Carter for a minute."

"Okay, Mom," he said, and climbed into the car.

"What's your week like?" I asked.

"I work full time, so I'm usually home by six after I pick Mav up from daycare."

"You don't work tomorrow, right?" I was having a difficult time not touching her, but I understood her need to go slow with Maverick around.

She smiled. "No, I make it a point not to work on Sundays."

"We're gonna do something, then."

"We are, are we?"

I nodded. "And Monday, and Tuesday, and Wednesday... getting the picture?"

Cassidy giggled. "Yes, I'm getting the picture, but I have a busy week, so I can't promise we'll see each other every day."

"Yeah, you can."

"Carter, I can't just drop everything in my life because you decree we will spend every waking moment together. I dance on Mondays, Mav has karate on Tuesday nights, then swimming on Thursday nights. Not to mention, by the time I've worked a full day, picked him up from daycare, cooked dinner, bathed, and put him to bed, I'm usually collapsing into bed myself. Maybe we can just plan the weekend after next."

"Hell, no. I'm not waiting that long, Cass."

"Well, I'm driving down to my parents on Friday night, so I don't know when else we'll manage it."

"Fuck!" I snapped.

Cassidy growled in frustration. "Six-year-old kid right there, buddy."

I squeezed the bridge of my nose.

"I should go," she said.

"Baby, wait." I slid my hand to her neck. "Tomorrow, we'll sit down and figure it all out."

"What if I have plans tomorrow?"

"Then you need to change them."

"Ohmigod, Carter, you are an idiot."

I grinned, leaning down to kiss her. She pushed at my chest, but I wouldn't budge. We were close enough to the car that, even if Maverick cared about anything other than his video game, he'd only see my side. I broke the kiss and stroked her cheek. "I'm bringin' you breakfast."

"You don't even know where I live."

I chuckled. "What does Mav like to eat?"

"He's a six-year-old boy. What did you like to eat when you were six?"

"Anything with sugar."

"Well, there you go. Nothing's changed."

"I'll be at your place at seven," I said.

"If you are, I will maim you."

"Nine, then."

Cassidy threw her hands in the air. "Fine. Come at nine, but as soon as you get there, you can watch Maverick while I go back to bed."

I dropped my head back and laughed. "Okay, baby. Whatever you want."

"I really should go, Carter. I hate driving this late."

"Want me to drive you?"

"No, it's okay." She smiled up at me. "I need a little time to process."

I stroked her cheek and kissed her quickly. "Text me when you're inside and safe."

"I'll try."

"Do."

She rolled her eyes. "Still bossy."

"Still stubborn," I retorted.

Cassidy sighed. "I'll see you tomorrow."

I nodded and watched her climb into her car and drive away.

SEVEN

Cassidy

AFTER I PUT Maverick to bed, I sat for quite a while on the sofa just staring off into space. I was still blind-sided by the events of the day and wasn't entirely sure if I hadn't dreamed it all. I heard my phone peal from my purse and frowned. It was almost eleven, I couldn't imagine who would be calling me at this hour.

I didn't reach it in time, but it started ringing again, so I answered it without looking at the caller ID. "Hello?"

"Fuck, Cass, I've been worried sick. Are you home?"

"Oh, Carter. Sorry. I totally forgot to text you."

"Yeah, I know." He sighed. "Are you okay?"

"I'm fine." I smiled. "I *have* managed to get myself home all by myself for the last seven years or so."

"Well, open your door. I want to see for myself."

"Shut up."

"Babe, open the door, yeah?"

"You're not really here, are you?"

"I'm really here, staring at apartment number seven-eighty-two."

"I'm seven-eighty-four."

"You are not," he countered.

"No, you're right, I'm not." I sighed and checked the peephole, before pulling open the door. "Hi," I said, and hung up.

Carter grinned, leaning down to kiss me as he pushed me back into my apartment and closed the door. "Hey," he said, between kisses, cupping my cheeks as he held me captive. "God damn, you can kiss."

I smiled against his lips and broke our connection. "So can you. But what are you doing here?"

"I was worried about you. I've called you sixty-two times."

"What? You did not."

"Okay, no. Three," he admitted, and turned to lock the door. "But when you didn't call me after the last one, I headed up."

"Carter, you can't stay. I'm sorry I worried you, but you can't just show up when you want to pound your chest and get all alpha male on me." I was really glad I got the words out, and I think they sounded legit. Of course, I didn't mean any of them. I was beyond flattered that he'd checked on me and I didn't want him to leave... ever.

"Yeah, I can," he said, and cocked his head. "Babe, you're gonna have to get used to this. I will do my best not to get possessive, but making sure you and Maverick are okay isn't negotiable."

I slid my arms around his waist and settled my cheek against his chest. "Okay."

He chuckled and gave me a gentle squeeze. "I thought

that was gonna go a different way."

"I have missed you so much. Even if this doesn't work out, I prayed for just one more day of us time, so I'll take whatever I can get."

"Baby, it's gonna work out. I'm not going anywhere."

I nodded against his chest, drawing in his scent. There was something about the combination of the cologne he'd worn forever mixed with leather. "Are you still wearing Stetson?"

"Hmm-mm. You still love it?"

"Hmm-mm," I mimicked. "It smells even better on you now."

He'd worn the fragrance for as long as I could remember, it had been a gift from an old girlfriend, but we'd both agreed it suited him perfectly.

He kissed the top of my head. "That's good to know."

"I have a confession," I breathed.

"Not sure I can handle another one of those in my life, honey," he joked.

I slapped his arm and leaned back. "Jerk."

He grinned. "What's your confession?"

"Huh-uh," I retorted, walking into the kitchen. "You lost your chance."

Carter chuckled as he followed me. "I have ways of making you talk. Have you forgotten?"

"Um, hello, we're not in the pond now, and I'm fully clothed. That was the last time I wore a string bikini in your presence."

"But you sang like a canary in order to get the bra back." He frowned. "I was kind of bummed you did. I only took it because I wanted a gander at the girls."

I gasped. "Ohmigod, you did not."

"I absolutely did." He grinned, leaning down to kiss me again.

I pushed his face away. "I don't even remember what the secret was."

"Me neither," he admitted. "But I didn't care, to be honest."

"This is weird. You get that right?"

"Weird, no. Different, yes." He gave me space and leaned against the counter. "Most people would kill to start a romance with half the foundation we've built, Cass."

"That *is* true," I mused.

"Mom?" Maverick called. "Mommy!"

I pushed away from Carter and rushed to Maverick's room. "Hey, baby, you okay?"

"I'm wet," he whispered. "I'm sorry."

"Aw, honey, you've got nothing to be sorry for. Remember? Sometimes this happens, it's no big deal."

He threw his arms around my neck and squeezed. "I love you, Mommy."

"Mmm, I love you too. Okay, kiddo, let's get you cleaned up and we'll change your bed. Uncle Carter is here, so don't worry if you hear voices."

"'K," he said, and grabbed clean clothes before heading to the bathroom.

"Where are the sheets, babe?" Carter asked from the doorway.

"In the hall. Closet's on the right." I stripped the bed and threw the sheets in the corner. He'd need a new mattress cover, so I leaned in the hall to tell Carter, stopping myself as I watched him hunkered down eye-to-eye with Maverick.

"Mommy never gets mad," Maverick said.

"Do you think she *should* get mad?"

He shrugged.

Carter laid a hand on his shoulder. "You know, bud, there's nothing to be ashamed about. It happens."

"Does it happen to you?" Maverick asked.

I bit back a smile as I watched the exchange.

"Not anymore, but it did when I was your age."

"Really?"

Carter nodded. "Yeah, and my mom never got mad either. Because it's no big deal."

"Ethan says only babies wet their pants."

"Who's Ethan?"

Ugh, Ethan. He was a nasty little kid in Maverick's daycare and he's the first six-year-old I'd ever wanted to cold cock into next year.

"He sits next to me sometimes during snack. He was teasing Xavier because he didn't make it to the potty on time." Maverick rubbed his eyes. "He made Xavier cry."

"Well, that wasn't very nice of Ethan, huh? But you don't need to worry about him, because he sounds like a bully," Carter said. "And you want to know a secret about bullies?"

Maverick nodded, his eyes wide in anticipation.

"Bullies are just cowards."

"What's a coward?"

"A coward is someone who is scared, which I have no problem with, but a bully is someone who won't admit he's scared and, instead of asking for help, he's mean so he can look strong."

Maverick's head bobbed up and down. "Oh, yeah, he's really mean sometimes."

"He is?" Carter's voice dropped low and I felt his anger pour off of him.

"Hmm-mmm, he pulls girls' hair and sometimes hits them."

"And do you pull girls' hair or hit them?"

Maverick gasped. "No! I wouldn't do that. Girls are pretty."

I grinned. Score one for Cassidy's parental powers.

"They *are* pretty," Carter agreed.

Maverick lowered his voice. "And sometimes, Katie lets me kiss her by the bathroom."

There just went my point. Damn it.

Carter chuckled. "Well, I think it would be a good rule to just plan on never hitting a girl even if she isn't pretty, and maybe it would also be a good rule to wait until you're older to kiss a girl."

"How come?"

"Because when you grow up to be a man, you have a responsibility to protect a woman, but more importantly, you need to respect a woman instead of just trying to kiss her."

"Are you going to protect my mom?"

"Absolutely," Carter said.

Maverick's grin grew, and he threw his arms around Carter's neck. "I'll help."

Carter chuckled and hugged him back. "I'd appreciate that, buddy."

I had to back into Mav's room again and force back tears. Ohmigod, was there anything more precious? The answer was no, and I'd spent six years missing out on it.

"Cass?" Carter walked into Maverick's room with fresh sheets. "Hey? You okay?"

"Hmm-mm," I said, brightly, refusing to look at him.

I felt his front hit my back and his arm slid around my waist. "Hey," he whispered. "What's wrong?"

"Nothing," I rasped. "I need to get these sheets in the washer."

He let me go and I pulled myself together as I did busy work. By the time the bed was changed, and Maverick was tucked back in, I felt a little closer to myself again.

Carter followed me into the living room and pulled me down onto the sofa next to him. "Spill."

"What?" I played dumb.

He wrapped an arm around my shoulders and pulled me against his chest. "Babe, why were you crying?"

"Because it's apparently my day."

"Cassidy." He chuckled, kissing my temple. "Tell me the real reason."

"I was just hit by how much we've missed." I snuggled closer. "He doesn't spend as much time with strong men for obvious reasons, well, other than my dad, of course, so having you say those things held weight. It doesn't matter how many times I tell him I will never get mad, he worries."

"Does he do that a lot?"

"No, but he does a couple times a year. Doctor says it's normal."

"Yeah, baby, it is. Were you worried it wasn't?"

I looked up at him and grimaced. "A little bit."

Carter smiled. "I'm gonna tell you something and you have to promise never to repeat it."

"I promise."

"Aidan wet the bed until he was ten."

I sat up. "Seriously?"

Carter nodded. "He just had a small bladder, so it was harder for him to make it to the head, but then it seemed to fix itself. I shared a room with him, so Mom told me if I ever teased him or told the other boys, she'd scalp me."

"Ohmigod, she totally would."

He grinned. "Which is why I never said a word."

I snuggled back against him. "You're also a nice guy, Carter, so that could be part of the reason."

"That's not for public knowledge."

"I'll take it to my grave," I promised.

"'Preciate it, baby." He kissed my temple. "You really don't date?"

"I really don't. The club get-together was my first... um... what would you call it? Attempt to see if I could find someone, maybe?"

"Yeah, well, you found someone."

I smiled. "Yes, I guess I did, huh?"

"You gonna let me stay?"

I sighed, dropping my head back to look at him. "I don't know."

"I'm stayin'."

I rolled my eyes. "What was the point of asking me if you've made up your mind?"

"Gotta give you some semblance of control, babe."

"You're an idiot."

He pushed me onto my back and stretched out on top of me. "An idiot who's going to make you want to scream." His mouth went to my neck and I couldn't help but crane it to give him better access.

"No screaming," I whispered. "I don't scream, but even if I did, I think we should wait a bit for this."

"You'll scream with me."

"Highly doubtful."

Carter dropped his head to my shoulder with a sigh.

"Carter, Maverick is only a few feet away. I want to try and at least *pretend* I'm not a total whore."

His eyes met mine and he scowled. "You ever say anything like that again, Cassidy Dennis, you and I are gonna have a problem."

"Well, it's true."

"It's not fuckin' true," he snapped. "Even if you fucked me in your kitchen right now, you'd still not be a whore. We love each other, we've known each other for over eighteen years, and we've been best friends for most of that time. I think we've waited for an appropriate amount of time, don't you?"

I shivered. "I'd kind of like the kitchen option at some point."

He groaned. "You seriously sayin' shit like that while tellin' me I gotta wait?"

"Sorry," I grumbled. "You're right."

"We can wait, baby, but I'm not leavin'."

"What do we tell Mav?"

"We tell him I'm home from the Air Force now, I've served my time and I'm gonna be a permanent feature in your lives. You've already established me in your home with all the photos."

I bit my lip. "That's actually really good."

"I know it's good. Shit, Cass, give me some credit."

"No." I wrinkled my nose. "You already have the upper

hand."

"Good to know." Carter grinned. "You gonna confess now?"

"Confess?" I asked. "Oh, that."

"Yes, that."

"Um...well, I have your cologne."

"Come again?"

I felt the heat crawl up my neck. "I was having a particularly bad day a few years ago, so I bought your cologne... it doesn't *quite* smell like you, but I have that old Harley T-shirt of yours, so every now and then I spray it and sleep with it." I covered my face with my hands. "Ohmigod, I can't believe I'm telling you this."

"You spray my shirt?"

I nodded, my hands still over my face.

He tugged my hands down and stroked my cheek. "I love you."

"You don't think I'm weird?"

"No," he said, but his head bobbed up and down.

"Dork."

He laughed. "You *are* weird, but not because of that."

"Well, that's a relief," I droned, sarcastically.

"I wondered where that damn shirt went."

I giggled. "I kind of stole it."

"I'm pickin' up on that." He cocked his head. "When?"

"The day before I left for Paris. I took it with me."

"You did?"

I nodded. "I'm sorry, Carter. I wish... I wish..."

"Huh-uh. Not going there, baby."

"Okay." I swallowed.

He smiled. "Go to bed, Cassidy. I'll sleep out here."

"I'll get you a blanket and pillow."

Carter kissed me again and then slid off me. "Thanks."

I rose to my feet and grabbed the bedding from the hall closet, forcing myself not to let down my guard. I wanted nothing more than to spend the night with Carter, but we needed to ease Maverick into things and I was grateful Carter understood that.

When I walked back into the living room, Carter had removed his boots and vest, and set his wallet and keys on the coffee table. I saw the old Ford key chain, now worn a little, but still as I remembered. "Do you still have the truck?"

"Yeah," he said. "You're surprised?"

I shrugged. "A little, I guess."

"We restored it together, Cass. Won't ever let it go."

I felt my stomach flip and I smiled. "Did you ever fix the door lock?"

"Yeah." He chuckled. "I'll take you and Maverick out tomorrow."

Handing him the pillow and blanket, I nodded. My emotions were all over the map, but I was too tired to analyze and figure them out. Carter dropped the bedding onto the sofa and reached out to pull me close. "Hey."

I blinked up at him.

"There is no pressure, yeah? We've done the hard part."

"I wish I believed you."

"What don't you believe?"

"That this is the hard part. We have so much baggage and I'm afraid it'll weigh us down moving forward."

"We have a couple of carry-ons, Cassidy." He stroked my pulse, his eyes boring into me. "I know there have been a few shitty circumstances that have kept us apart, but deep down, we're the same people, right?"

"I hope so."

"I'm here. I'm not going anywhere. We're gonna figure this out together and it's gonna be better than we ever expected."

I dropped my head to his chest. "You're still the eternal optimist I see."

"And you're still a worrywart."

"Promise me we're going to be okay."

He lifted my chin and nodded. "I'll make sure it is. Trust

me, okay?"

"I'll try."

Carter chuckled. "There's my girl."

"Okay, I'm leaving you now or it will never happen."

"You get lonely, wake me."

"No."

"No?"

I bit my lip. "I'm used to being lonely, Carter. But if I wake you and take you to bed, I will never let you out of it, and I need to make sure we do this right."

"Okay, baby." He leaned down and kissed me. "Love you."

"Love you too."

I headed off to bed, leaving my door open, which I rarely did. I liked knowing Carter was close and I don't remember ever sleeping so soundly.

EIGHT

Cassidy

THE SOUND OF rain pounding on my window, along with the unending laughter of my child, woke me with a start. I threw the covers off my body and sat up, my heart racing until I remembered that Carter was here.

I took a few seconds to listen through the closed door, wondering when that had happened. I could only assume Carter had closed it so I could sleep. I climbed out of bed and sneaked down the hall to the bathroom where I brushed my teeth and hair before following the sound of voices.

Arriving at the kitchen, I laid my hand over my chest, the scene so unbelievably adorable, it was almost as cute as a kitten hugging a puppy. Maverick was kneeling on a chair at the counter, whisking batter in a bowl while Carter stood at the stove, cracking eggs over a pan.

"Mom," Maverick exclaimed. "I'm helping Carter with breakfast."

"I see that, baby." I closed the distance between us and he lifted his head for a kiss. I hoped he always wanted to kiss me in the morning. "You're doing such a good job."

"Hey, what about me?" Carter challenged.

"What about you?" I said.

He tugged me to him and covered my mouth with his. I mumbled against his lips in an effort to break our connection, but he slid his hand to the back of my head to hold me to him.

"Good morning," he whispered once he released me.

I narrowed my eyes at him and his response was a smug grin, so I wagged my finger and shook my head. "Behave."

"So, if you kiss Mommy, does that mean I can still kiss Katie?" Maverick asked.

"Busted," I mouthed.

Carter flipped the eggs and then faced Maverick. "Here's the deal, buddy. Mommy and me are gonna get married, so it's a little different."

"You're gonna get married?" he asked.

"Carter," I warned.

"Yeah, buddy, we are."

"Mav, will you please go to your room for a minute?" I said. "*Uncle* Carter and I need a second."

"Okay, Mama," he said, and jumped off the chair. He left the bowl on the counter and headed to his room.

"Are you kidding me with this?" I snapped.

"What?" Carter slid the eggs from the pan onto a plate.

He'd made himself comfortable in my kitchen and he looked good there. Damn it!

"You didn't think this might be something we'd discuss *first* and then decide how to tell Maverick *together*?" I crossed my arms. "You had no right to blindside me like that."

Carter flipped off the burner and leaned against the coun-

75

ter, thus beginning the first of many epic stare-off battles. His slow, sexy smile ultimately solidified my loss. Unable to continue to look at him in all his glory, I picked up the bowl Maverick had left and began to whisk the hell out the pancake batter.

"Babe."

Whisk, whisk.

"Cassidy."

"What?" I swiped the whisk around the side of the bowl and then began to beat it again, but found them gently removed from my hands and set next to the stove.

"The batter's done."

"Okay." I stepped to the sink and washed my hands.

"Cass, you need to look at me, baby."

I grabbed a towel and faced him, glancing up at him as I dried my hands.

"I'm sorry," he said. "You're right. We should have talked about it."

"Thank you."

"How would you like to proceed?"

"I think we should just move past it," I said.

Carter frowned. "We're not movin' past it, baby, so let's figure out what we want to say to Mav."

I set the towel on the counter. "Excuse me?"

Carter lit the stove again and started the pancakes. "I say we head down to the courthouse next week and take care of the legalities, I can have Mack draw up adoption paperwork, then we can talk to our families and go from there."

"I'm sorry, can you back up a little?" I requested.

"How far?"

"Carter Michael Quinn, you do not get to talk over me on this! I have not agreed to anything, especially considering the fact you haven't actually asked me anything…" I let out a frustrated squeak. "Stop looking at me like that!"

"Like what, baby?"

Carter had always had this annoying tactic of barreling

over me with his dominant personality and he'd usually get his way, but I was older and wiser now and wasn't going to let him do it to me again. "Get out."

He chuckled and flipped a pancake.

"I mean it, Carter, get out of my house."

"And why would you want me to do that?" he challenged.

"Because you're being..." I lowered my voice, "...an overbearing ass! Out or I'm calling Jaxon."

"Why would you call Jaxon?"

"Because he's the only one I can think of who has the power to bodily remove you."

Carter chuckled. "Call him, then."

I huffed and turned away from him, making a valiant attempt at removing the nonstick coating from one of my baking sheets. Not the smartest thing I'd ever done, but I needed somewhere to focus my annoyance.

Carter set the pan at the back of the stove again and turned the water off, handing me a towel. "You done?"

"No."

"Babe, you're not gonna call Jaxon and I'm not going anywhere. We're gonna talk about this and then it's done."

I felt tears of frustration well up in my eyes and fisted my hands at my side.

"Cassidy." Carter sighed and pushed away from the counter. "I didn't mean to make you cry."

"You know I only cry when I'm pissed. I can't out talk you when I'm flustered, and doing that to me in front of Maverick was totally unfair."

He wrapped his arms around me, despite the fact mine were still at my side. "I know. That wasn't my intention, I just didn't want you to say no."

"I haven't been asked anything to say no to!"

Before Carter could charm me further, my phone pealed, and I stepped away from him to grab it, seeing Kevin's name pop up on the screen. "Hey, Kev."

"Hey," he said brightly. "We on for tomorrow? I never got a response."

"Ohmigod, Kevin, I'm so sorry. Yes, definitely. Seven, right?"

"Perfect. I'll see you tomorrow."

"'Bye." I hung up and set my phone back on the counter.

"Mom, can I come out now?" Maverick called.

Crap, I'd forgotten about Mav.

I jabbed a finger at Carter. "Conversation shelved but not over, got it?"

He gave me a cocky grin. "Yeah, baby, got it."

"Come have breakfast, honey."

"Whoo hoo!" he sang, and rushed to one of the stools at the island.

Carter set pancakes and eggs in front of him while I grabbed syrup, and then we joined Maverick and finished our breakfast without any drama.

"Maverick, go wash up, okay?" Carter said, and Maverick jumped down from the island.

"Hands and face, please," I called to his back.

"Okay, Mom."

"How about we hang out, watch a movie, or play a game?" Carter suggested.

"It's not like we can go anywhere I guess."

"That's the spirit," Carter droned, and smiled. "Am I forgiven?"

"Yes, of course you are."

He kissed me, and we went about our day.

* * *

Monday was a typical Monday, I guess, with the added bonus of pouring down rain again… in June. That was the Pacific Northwest for you. Carter had offered to take Maverick for the day, rather than me taking him to daycare, which meant, I got an extra hour of sleep that morning, which made for a happy Cassidy. And Maverick was beside himself with

78

excitement to do "man stuff." I didn't know what "man stuff" would entail, but Carter assured me there would be burping, farting, and general uncleanliness involved, so I left it at that.

I'd had a rather long day at work, considering I was forced into a meeting with several other analysts and we had to video conference with our New York office. Good God, I hated meetings, but we were being "introduced" to the new Vice President of Accounts and we all had to look like we cared. It was exhausting. The new guy seemed nice. Thomas Dale was British and attractive, I think... at least that's what I was told. We were having issues with the feed, so New York could see us, but we saw them for all of five minutes. The office girls were all aflutter with him, but all I cared about was the stack of work waiting for me.

I'd been back at my desk for almost an hour when I got a phone call from the new VP. A little strange, since I wouldn't have much to do with him, but I took the call anyway.

"I just wanted to take a moment to thank you for your time," Tom said.

"No problem," I said.

"Do you have any feedback for me?"

"On what?"

"The meeting, how it went. Perhaps something you feel needs to change."

The question was strange as I had nothing to do with his department, but there were always ways to improve working conditions.

"Yes, actually, I have a few ideas."

"Excellent," he said. "Why don't you shoot me an email with your thoughts and I'll look them over. I'll be visiting next week, and I'd love to take you to lunch if you have time."

I pushed a stack of files aside. "I have no idea what my week will be like, but I don't typically have much time for lunch."

"Well, I hope you'll find the time for me. I must run, but have a lovely day, Cassidy."

He hung up and I sat staring at my phone for a second, a little shocked by the strange conversation. I shrugged and formalized my ideas as I moved through my day. Before I left, I sent a quick email to Tom and then shut down my computer.

I arrived home to find Carter had cooked. Seriously, I was loving this side of him. I hated to cook, so if he wanted to take that on, I was all for it. The only issue I had was I was dancing in less than an hour and I never ate before a strenuous workout, so Carter wrapped it up and set it in the fridge for later.

"Maverick usually comes with me on dance nights," I explained as I slipped off my shoes and hung up my rain-coat. "So, you're free."

"I don't want to be free," Carter said.

"You don't mind watching him?" I asked, walking into my bedroom.

"I was thinkin' we'd both come with you."

I glanced over my shoulder with a snort. "You hate bal-let."

"No, I don't."

"Since when?" I grabbed my dance bag and a clean leo-tard and tights from my drawer.

"Okay, I still hate ballet... but I love watching you."

I grinned. "It'll bore you, honey. Trust me."

He leaned against the doorframe and crossed his arms. "Why are you doin' this?"

"What do you mean?"

"I thought you weren't dancing anymore."

I made sure my toe shoes were in the bag and frowned at Carter. "I never said that."

"Maverick did."

"No, he didn't. He said I don't do it as often as I like, but

I still dance." I studied Carter's expression. He looked irritated. "Kevin's working out a new routine and I'm helping him with it. He's doing some showcase in September and his regular partner's in San Francisco until August."

He scowled. "Does he do shit like lift you above his head while his hands are on your pus—"

"Carter!"

"Just answer the question."

"Ohmigod, no I won't. You're taking this to a level it doesn't need to go." I closed the distance between us and laid my hand in the middle of his chest. "Now, go amuse yourself while I get changed."

He backed away, but I could see he didn't like it. I changed quickly, threw sweats over my dance stuff and walked into the living room.

"Mav, take over the game for a bit, yeah?" Carter said, rising to his feet.

"Okay," he said, and focused back on the television.

Carter slid my bag from my shoulder, his other hand at my waist, pushing me gently back toward my room.

"What are you doing?"

He closed us in and wrapped his arms around me, leaning down to kiss me as he guided me to the bed. Without warning, the front of my leotard and bra were pulled down, exposing my breasts. I moaned when Carter drew a nipple into his mouth, then focused on the other one.

Cupping my breasts together, he gently blew on the sensitive nubs before giving them each a gentle nip and righting my clothes.

"What are you doing?" I rasped.

"I wanted my mouth to be the last thing you remembered before he put is grubby hands on your body."

"Ohmigod." I bit back a groan. "You're an idiot."

"Mom!"

"Just a second, buddy," I called. "We'll be right out."

"Can I have some juice?"

"Sure." I wrinkled my nose. "Do you see why we can't do this?"

"We'll have our time," he promised.

"I'm a single parent, Carter. I don't have those times often, if ever."

"Well, you're not a single parent anymore." He slipped his hand to my neck and squeezed. "We'll make time."

"Easy for you to—"

His kiss cut off my retort and my focus was once again drawn to what he could do with his tongue. Good lord, the man could kiss. He rolled a nipple between his fingertips before breaking our connection and dropping his forehead to mine. "You gonna remember who your man is?"

"And who's that?"

"Cassidy," he growled.

Two could play this game. I slid my hand to cup him on the outside of his jeans, smiling when he hissed against my neck. "I had a feeling you'd be big," I breathed. "Wasn't quite expecting that though."

He chuckled. "You know exactly what to say to a man."

"Just speaking the truth, Carter." I smiled. "You're almost as big as Kevin."

"What the fuck!" he bellowed, and knifed off the bed.

I dissolved into giggles and I heard him swear again, and then his hands were at my waist and I was being tickled mercilessly.

"Carter!" I squealed.

"Say Uncle, Cassidy."

"You know Kevin's cup is an extra-large."

He squeezed my middle again and I squealed.

"Say Uncle!" he demanded.

My door popped open and Maverick stood at the threshold looking worried as he asked, "Mom? Are you okay?"

Carter released me immediately and I sat up, waving Maverick over. "I'm fine honey. Uncle Carter was just making me giggle."

Maverick let out a sigh of relief and rushed to the bed. "What were you doing, Uncle Carter?"

Carter grabbed Maverick and pulled him onto the bed, starting the tickle attack he'd just laid on me. "This."

Maverick howled with laughter and I couldn't help but join in the fun.

"Okay, okay," Maverick cried in between laughs. "Stop!"

We stopped and the three of us lay sideways across my bed trying to catch our breath.

"Can we play Hot Wheels now, please?" Maverick asked.

Carter had showed up with a little video game surprise for Maverick, which now firmly placed Carter in the favorite of anyone category.

Carter chuckled. "Yeah, let's go."

We moved as a group into the living room and I grabbed my bag, purse, and keys. "Bed time eight o'clock," I ordered, leaning down to kiss Maverick. "No arguments."

"Okay, Mom."

"I'll just walk your mom out, Mav," Carter said.

"'K."

Carter walked me to the door and laid another kiss that had my breath coming in short bursts. "Mine," he decreed, as he cupped my breasts and kissed me again.

I giggled. "Yeah, yeah."

"Cassidy."

"Don't worry, honey, you're the only man to cop a feel since I stopped breastfeeding. Relax."

He sighed. "I can still come with you."

"And risk a fall because I'm worried you'll kill Kevin if he touches me somewhere you don't approve of?"

"I don't approve of him touching you at all."

"I rest my case." I leaned up on my tiptoes and kissed him again. "I'll see you later."

"Drive safely."

"No. I'm going to ram my car into a tree."

"Cassidy," he hissed.

"Love you," I called, and headed to my car.

NINE

Cassidy

FRIDAY AFTER WORK, I loaded Maverick in the car and we made the three (plus) hour drive down to my parents'. Because Kevin wasn't available for our normal dance time next week, I'd taken advantage of that fact and taken Monday and Tuesday off work. My sisters would be at home as well, so I was looking forward to quality time with the family. What I wasn't looking forward to was not seeing Carter.

He'd called just before I left and hearing his voice made me miss him before I'd even left. He'd stayed Monday night, but our schedules for the rest of the week meant I only saw him briefly on Thursday as well, but he couldn't stay. I hated to admit it, but if I could have finagled a way to bow out of the trip, I might have considered it if it meant I got two days alone with him.

Traffic had been light, so I arrived a little after eight-thirty. Maverick slept most of the way and I had to admit, I was pretty tired by the time I pulled up to the house... driving always did that to me. Even so, there was something cathartic about coming home. Even if I didn't want to move back to the small town, it was nice not to have to worry about the day-to-day grind. I would get to sleep in and that was huge.

Before I turned off the ignition, Dad walked toward the car and opened the back door.

"Hi, Daddy."

"Hey, honey. I'll take Mav up," he whispered, and unbuckled him.

"Thanks." I smiled and locked up, grabbing our stuff from the trunk and following them inside. Setting everything down in the foyer, I made my way to the kitchen. Mom was pulling cookies out of the oven while Shannon was pouring a glass of wine.

"Is that for me?" I asked hopefully.

Shannon giggled. "Yes, but hug first."

I obliged and then took the glass of wine from her. "Kids asleep?"

Shannon had married John Worth four years ago and now had two children, a son, Kai who was three and a daughter, Alana, who had just turned two.

"Yes, thank God," she said. "They were a little harder to corral today. Being a single parent is *hard*."

I giggled. "Tell me about it."

Mom hugged me and then shooed us out of the kitchen. I followed Shannon into the family room.

"Maverick's so big," Shannon said, sitting on the sofa. "I got to kiss his head before Dad swept him off to bed."

"I know. Mav's looking forward to playing with the cousins and I'm dying to see Kai and Alana... they probably don't even look the same."

John and Shannon had moved to California for his job over a year ago, which we all hated, but the money was far too good to pass on. Shannon promised they'd be back one day and I secretly hoped it was soon.

Shannon grinned. "They seem to change daily."

"When does John arrive?"

"He'll be here Sunday night. He had a few things to finish up, so will be catching a flight in the morning and grabbing a car at the airport."

"Mia's coming tomorrow, right? She texted me last week, but nothing since."

"New boy haze." Shannon sipped her wine.

"Ohmigod, I know. I wonder how long this one will last."

"Let's hope longer than a week," Mom retorted as she joined us. "I'm too old to keep up with the changing lovers."

I wrinkled my nose. "Ew, Mom, please never say lover again."

Mom grinned. "Loverrrrrr."

Shannon and I dissolved into giggles.

"What's so funny?" Dad asked, strolling in and sitting next to Mom.

"I was discussing Mia's boyfriends," Mom said.

"Let's not." Dad groaned. "She's going to kill me, that one."

"Mav go down alright?" I asked.

"Didn't even stir."

"Thanks, Dad."

The rest of the evening was spent catching up, but by ten I couldn't keep my eyes open, so I headed up to bed.

* * *

The next morning (okay, it was just past noon, but I'd slept in, so for the sake of argument, it was morning), I was sitting at the table with my coffee when I heard the screen door slam. Shannon and my dad were in the back yard with the kids and Mom was in the kitchen.

"Lucy, I'm hoooome," Mia called in her best Desi Arnaz impersonation.

"In here," I responded, and met her halfway, pulling her in for a hug. "Hey there gorgeous."

"Hey, Sassidy." Mia grinned. "Ohmigod, you're never going to guess what I heard!"

"Hug me first, then gossip," Mom ordered.

Mia did as she was told and, once she grabbed herself a coffee, sat with me at the table. "Carter Quinn's home."

I gasped, drawing hot liquid down my throat and choking as I tried to breathe.

"You okay?" Mom asked, rushing over with a glass of water.

"Wrong pipe," I rasped as I slapped my chest. "What do you mean, he's home?" I asked, once I got my breath back.

"Like, he drove into town early this morning and stopped at the Smiths' flower shop to pick up something for his mom," Mia continued. "He told them he was home for a few days."

Once Carter had left the day of my confession, he hadn't been back. I knew this only because Mia told me. Even when there was a huge Quinn reunion, he'd stayed away, which I'd always found sad. But since I'd never asked him about it (partly because I didn't want to find out the reason he hadn't been back was because of me), I was able to put it out of my mind.

"Well, this *is* news," Mom mused, and smiled at me. "Interesting."

My stomach flipped to think he'd changed his plans to come home knowing I'd be here, but I played dumb. "Is it?"

"Very." Mom raised an eyebrow.

"Mom!" Maverick called, running in, his face red with excitement. "I caught a frog."

He opened his palm and Mia shrieked as the frog jumped

at her. She spilled her coffee in her haste to escape the amphibian, and Maverick slid under the table in an effort to catch it. I made a run for paper towels while Mia hid behind my mother, who was laughing hysterically.

I rounded the counter, paper towels in hand, and came to screeching halt when I caught sight of Carter standing in the doorway of the kitchen. Mia gasped, my mom stopped laughing, and Maverick cried, "Uncle Carter!"

"Hey, buddy."

"I caught a frog!"

"You did?" He smiled down at him.

"*Don't* open your hand, Mav," I rushed to say, and laid the towels over the spill. "Show him outside."

Maverick nodded and ran back outside, Carter following.

"Ohmigod," Mia said. "What the hell is Carter Quinn doing here?"

"I have a feeling he's here for your sister," Mom mused.

"Since when?"

I sighed and threw the paper towels in the trash. "It's a long story," I admitted.

Before more could be said on the subject, Carter returned, a bouquet of flowers in his hand and a smug, but adorable smile on his face.

"These are for you, Wendy," he said, and handed the spring flowers to her (Mom's favorite, I might add).

"Oh, Carter, that's so sweet," she crooned, and hugged him. "Thank you! I'll just get a vase."

"Hey, Mia," he continued.

"Carter."

He smiled. "You look great."

She didn't respond. She just crossed her arms and glared. "What are you doing here, Carter?" Mia had always been my protector and even though we weren't kids anymore, she still fell into the role on occasion.

"Mia," Mom admonished. "Be nice."

"Hi Carter. Good to see you. You've changed," Mia said, her voice somewhat monotone. "What are you doing here?"

"Was in the area… thought I'd come say hi."

"Hi," she said. "'Bye."

"He just got here," I countered.

"So? The guy takes off like a hundred years ago and shows up just when you happen to be here for a few days?" She faced him and frowned. "I hope it's not to hurt Cassidy again."

"Mia!" I snapped.

"What? I don't trust him."

My mouth dropped open. "He didn't do anything wrong."

"He hurt you!" she argued.

"Because of what I did!"

"Cassidy," Carter warned.

"Ohmigod, don't talk to her like that," Mia snapped.

"Mia, it's fine."

"It's fine for him to growl at you?"

"You don't understand—"

Mia gasped. "You're seeing him! Ohmigod, you're totally seeing him again and you didn't tell me!"

"I—"

"Whatever!" she snapped, and stormed out of the room.

I gave Carter a look of desperation and he just chuckled, sliding his hand to my neck and pulling me close. I tried to pull away. "My mom—"

"Left the room ten minutes go," he interrupted.

I craned my neck to see that the kitchen was in fact empty, before wrapping my arms around him and giving him a squeeze. "What are you doing here?"

"No way in hell I'm going an entire weekend, let alone five days, without seeing you two," he whispered.

My heart warmed when he included Maverick in that statement. "Crazy man."

He chuckled, lifting my chin and kissing me.

"Mom!" Maverick called. "There's a dog outside, can I play with it?"

"She's mine, buddy," Carter said. "Let me introduce you and then you can play with her."

"You have a dog?" I asked, unsure if I wanted to let my kid play with a strange animal.

"Yeah," Carter said, and tugged me toward the front door. "She's a black lab. Super friendly, but excitable. She won't hurt you, so don't worry."

"Where's she been while you've been with us?"

"Jaxon or Aidan take her if I need them to, but otherwise, she's pretty much with me wherever I go."

I nodded and followed Carter to the front door where Maverick waited. Carter pushed open the screen door and the dog whined and shook her tail, but overall seemed pretty chill.

"Hey, girl," Carter crooned. "I got some people for you to meet. Sit. Stay." She did exactly what he told her to do and then Carter guided Maverick forward. "Whenever you see a dog, you should always make sure an adult is with you, okay? Never walk up to it by yourself."

Maverick nodded. "'K."

"Stand really still and hold your hand out like this to let her smell you so she knows who you are."

Maverick did as he directed, and the dog sniffed him, her tail wagging a mile a minute.

"Good job," Carter said.

"Can I give her a treat?" Maverick asked.

"I've got some treats in my bag which I left inside. Let's go grab them," Carter said, and smiled at me. "You okay?"

"Yep. It's all good."

While Carter took Maverick back inside, I introduced myself to the dog, looking at her collar and then needing a minute to compose myself.

"Mav, if you throw the ball, she'll get it for you," Carter said, as they returned to the porch. "Just keep it close, okay?"

Maverick nodded and led the dog onto the driveway.

"Cass?" Carter asked.

"Hmm?"

He turned me to face him and frowned. "Hey, what's wrong?"

"You didn't think to warn me?"

"About?"

"The fact you named your dog Cassidy?"

Carter chuckled. "I thought about it, but then I wasn't quite sure how to approach the subject."

"Why?"

"I would think that would be obvious."

"Tell me anyway," I pressed.

He slid his hand to my waist and pulled me closer. "One of the girls at the shop volunteers at the humane society and someone dropped off a litter of puppies. Don't know where they came from, but she called me because I mentioned I was lookin' to get a dog. When I had a night off, I went down, and this tiny little thing had figured out how to finagle her way out of the box they were in and she decided my boot was her play thing. I was still wearing them. She was the only girl, and I hadn't really thought to get a girl, but she followed me everywhere and would whine if I was separated from her. I picked her up and she fell asleep against my chest. The rest is history. I couldn't take her home that night because she wasn't quite ready, but I visited every day and took her home as soon as I could." He stroked my cheek. "What else could I name the little girl who was tiny and clever and fearless? There'd only been one other female who'd wrapped herself around my heart, and I missed her."

"Ohmigod," I breathed and dropped my head onto his chest. He held me for a few precious seconds before Cassidy stuck her nose between us. I giggled and knelt down to pet her. "Well, that sure beats me being a bitch, huh, girl?"

Carter roared with laughter before leaning down to kiss

me. "God, I love you."

"Stop being all sappy and crap." I blinked back tears.

"Yes, dear," he quipped.

Maverick jogged up the steps. "Mom, can I swim?"

"If Grandad's with you?"

"I'll find him."

"If he is, then, yes. Go get your suit on."

"You gonna swim too, Uncle Carter?" Maverick asked.

"Not today, buddy, but maybe another time. We can head to the pond."

"'K." He rushed back into the house as Carter released me.

"Want coffee?" I asked, and led Carter back into the house. The dog stayed on the porch.

"No, babe. I need to head back. Mom's losing her mind right now."

I faced him again. "In a good way?"

He shrugged.

"Maybe you shouldn't have come. I know she blames me—"

"Stop," he said, and closed the distance between us, pulling me to him again. "None of this is about you."

"How can you say that?" I stared up at him. "I'm the one—"

"Damn it, Cassidy, it's done. We're not talkin' about it anymore."

I let out a frustrated groan. "We can't continue this trend, buddy. At some point, we need to deal with a few things."

"Not today."

I rolled my eyes, but nodded. "Fine, but soon."

His response was to kiss me. "I need to go. I'll call you later."

"Maybe I'll answer."

Carter chuckled and walked out the door.

"So?" Mom showed up again, fast enough to indicate she'd probably been listening from the dining room. She put the vase of flowers on the kitchen table and faced me. "When did *that* start?"

I sighed. "Less than a week ago."

"Have a seat, honey. Let's talk." She took one herself and smiled. "Your dad's keeping everyone outside for a bit."

I sat down and dropped my forehead to my palm. "I don't really know what to tell you. I'm still not entirely sure what's going on."

"Start at the beginning and we'll sort it out from there."

I filled her in on the meeting at the club and our week so far, leaving out a few of the more graphic parts.

"Wow," she whispered.

"Yeah."

"It's really about time."

I raised my head. "What?"

Mom chuckled. "Honey, you've loved each other forever. I knew you'd have to find your way back to each other eventually."

"Didn't know psychic was in your wheelhouse," I grumbled.

"Don't need to be a psychic to know you're meant for each other, but if you want me to be more fabulous than I am, I'm good with that."

I giggled and then groaned. "I don't know why he's here."

"Aw, honey, he's here for you." She patted my arm. "And he's making that fact known in a pretty major way."

"How's that?"

"Cass, he hasn't been home in seven years. Not once. Do you know what that's done to his mom?"

"I can imagine." I frowned. "But they're still talking, right? Jaxon said they were."

"I think so."

I frowned. "But you don't know?"

"Honey, it's complicated."

"Uncomplicate it for me," I said.

94

"Sheila and I haven't talked in almost as long as Carter's been gone."

"What?" I gasped. "Why not? You were amazing friends."

"Well, I certainly thought we were, but she showed her true colors after he went off to the Air Force, and quite frankly, I didn't need the drama."

"Why didn't you tell me?" I asked.

"Because you didn't need to be roped into her craziness, honey. It had nothing to do with you, after all."

I sighed. "So, how do you know he never came home."

"Aidan kept me updated. He keeps in touch." Mom smiled. "Carter's been to the beach once, I guess, but other than that, nothing... until now." Mom smiled. "So, he's announcing to the world... at least our small one... that you're his and he's claiming you."

"Ohmigod, Mom, he is not."

"Yeah, honey, he is. Mark my words." She smiled. "Now, go read or swim or whatever you want. Mav's happy, so you get to rest."

"I don't even know what that means anymore."

Mom laughed. "I remember, honey."

I grabbed my Kindle, but before I let myself relax, I went in search of Mia. She was in her room, throwing things from her suitcase into her dresser.

"Hey, can we talk?" I asked from the doorway.

"Oh, we do that still?"

"Mia," I sighed. "Babe, this all happened, like, three days ago."

She raised an eyebrow.

"Hand to God," I said, and raised my hand. "Saturday, actually, so what's that? Six? I just happened to be at a party and he was there. I did text you on Sunday, but you didn't respond."

"Well, if you'd said the great Carter Quinn was sniffin' after your panties, I might have."

Mia was always colorful with her words. "Um... gross."

She giggled and threw her suitcase into her closet. "Well, I would have."

"It wasn't something I wanted to text bomb you with. I figured if you had time, you'd respond, and if not, I'd talk to you this weekend."

She sat on her bed and patted the mattress. "Assume the position."

I grabbed a pillow and we laid down facing each other.

"So, he was at a party. Details."

I filled her in on everything... and I mean everything. There really wasn't anything I kept from big sister Mia.

"Holy shit, Cass. The man finally pulled his head out of his ass? I don't believe it."

"Mia, I'm really the one to blame here."

"Bullshit."

I took a deep breath. "Okay, well, we both have culpability in this and he's apologized, I've apologized, and we are making a conscious effort to move forward. I've missed him, Mia."

"I know you have, honey." She smiled. "He went and got fuckin' *huge*."

"Tell me about it."

"Big dick?"

"Mia!" I knew I was beet red.

"What? It's a logical question. Did him getting bigger increase or decrease the size of his cock?"

"How would I know?"

"What do you mean? You haven't seen it?"

I rolled onto my back and ran my hands down my face with a groan. "Ohmigod, Mia. No, I haven't seen it."

"I'd have hoisted my sail up that mast and sailed the seven seas, or twelve. Let's go with twelve."

"Ohmigod." I giggled. "It'll happen. I just want to take it slow."

"Then fast, then slow again."

"Mia!"

She giggled as well and then took my hand. "He better do it right, Sass."

"He will. Now, if I could just get him to quit telling me we're getting married and put some kind of effort into asking me, we'd be good."

"He's talking marriage?"

I rolled to face her again. "He's talking, let's go down to the courthouse and take care of the legalities."

"Romantic." Mia rolled her eyes. "Douche."

"Don't call him a douche. He's not a douche." I smiled. "He's up to something."

"Oh really?"

I nodded. "Yep, he's just seeing if I blink first."

"Don't blink, Sass."

"Bitch, *please*. I don't blink."

Mia giggled. "There's hope for you yet."

"God, I hope so." I squeezed her hand. "Can I go read now? I need a time-out from my adorable but very busy little boy."

"I will go spend some time in the pool with my niece and nephews and let you and Shannon go on time-out."

"This is why we love you best."

Mia slid off the bed. "Don't you forget it."

I stayed where I was and powered up my Kindle. Mia's bed was more comfortable than mine anyway.

TEN

Cassidy

MAVERICK CRASHED AT about eight, which suited me just fine. He'd been nonstop all day and had tired himself out, as did my niece and nephew, which meant I got some quality time with my family without kids.

I headed up to my room about ten and found several texts from Carter on my phone. I'd left it on my dresser, partly on purpose, partly because I'd forgotten to retrieve it after my shower. Instead of texting him back, I called.

"Hey, baby," he said, sounding breathless.

"Hi, honey, you okay?"

"Was just finishing a run."

I slid my watch off. "Want to call me back?"

"Hell, no. I've missed your voice. Just give me a minute to cool down."

"Okay." I grinned. "I talked to Mia. Everything's good."

"I wasn't worried, babe."

"Well, I was," I countered.

He chuckled. "You worry too much, Cass."

"Just because I'm paranoid, doesn't mean no one's following me."

"Yeah, but I'm following *them*, so I got you, baby."

"Well, there is that." I smiled. "Are you really out running?"

"Treadmill."

"At ten o'clock at night?"

"Baby, you're not here, so I had to work off some pent-up energy."

I bit my lip... hard.

"Babe, you there?"

"Yes," I said, my voice husky. "I was just imagining how you might work off that pent up energy in other ways."

"I'm coming over."

"I don't know if I feel up to working off anything in my parents' house, Carter," I whispered.

"As much as that sucks, I agree with you, but I *am* gonna come say goodnight," he said. "Do I have to climb the tree?"

I giggled. "Do you *want* to climb the tree?"

"Not particularly, no."

"I'll meet you on the porch, then."

"I'll grab a shower and be there in a few."

"Okay, honey."

I hung up and headed to the bathroom to brush my teeth and freshen up a bit. I still had no makeup on and my hair was in a messy bun due to doing nothing all day. I combed it out, then pinched my cheeks for a little color rather than putting makeup on. I'd just have to take it off again, and quite frankly, I couldn't be bothered.

Carter texted me to let me know he was on his way, so I checked on Maverick who was sleeping soundly and then

99

slipped out of the house. It was rather cool, so I grabbed a blanket and sat on the porch swing to wait for him.

"Hey, baby," he said as he jogged up the steps. His hair was still damp, but he smelled delicious as he leaned down to kiss me.

"Hi."

He sat next to me and wrapped an arm around my shoulders, pulling me close. "Missed you today."

"Me too." I smiled up at him. "How'd it all go after you left here?"

"Fine."

"Fine, good, or fine, meh?"

He sighed. "Babe, I'm gonna say somethin' and then you need to drop it."

I pushed away from him and sat up. "Well, that sounds crappy."

"The shit I'm dealin' with with my family has nothin' to do with you. I know you think you've caused a rift or some shit like that, but it's not true."

"So, your mom doesn't blame me for you leaving?"

"It doesn't matter."

"It does to me," I said, and stood. "How can we make a life together if your parents' hate me?"

"They don't hate you, Cass."

I crossed my arms. "Let me tell you a little secret about boys and their mamas. We are vicious when someone hurts them, and I can guarantee that your mother sees me as the enemy in regard to you... especially, because I took you away from her."

He smiled and rose to his feet. "Baby, you didn't take me away from her. And my mom might be working some shit out in her head, but she does not hate you. But even if she did, it wouldn't matter. I choose you and I will *every* time. She knows that."

Well, that was seriously nice.

"She does?" I whispered.

"Yeah, honey, she does." He pulled me into his arms and gave me a gentle squeeze. "I love you, Cassidy. It's always been you."

"I kinda love you too."

He chuckled, and I dropped my head back to smile up at him. He covered my lips with his as I stood on my tiptoes and opened my mouth, touching my tongue to his and deepening the kiss. Breaking the kiss, he cupped my face and stroked my cheek. "I can't wait to wake up with you every morning."

I grinned. "You think that'll happen?"

"Hell, yeah, it'll happen. I still say we head to the courthouse sooner than later."

"You're an idiot."

"Why am I an idiot?" he challenged.

I pulled away from him, but he held tight. "The fact you don't know why just happens to drive home that you are."

"I'm gonna wear you down, Cassidy, you'll see."

I rolled my eyes. "How long are you staying?"

"Tonight or this weekend?"

"This weekend," I clarified.

"I'm driving home with you."

"What?"

"You let me know when you're ready to go and I'll drive home."

"What about your truck... or bike, or whatever you drove down with?"

He smiled. "I came with Jaxon. He's leaving on Monday."

I dropped my cheek to his chest. "Are you telling me that you came down this weekend because of me and that I don't have to drive all the way home by myself?"

Carter chuckled. "Yeah, baby, that's what I'm telling you."

I squeezed his middle. "Sometimes, Carter Quinn, I love you so much I think I might explode."

He laughed and kissed my head. "Well, don't do that... it's messy."

I grinned and nodded.

"You gonna make out with me a little more before I have to leave?"

Smiling up at him, I licked my lips. "Um, duh."

He led me back to the swing and the make out session commenced.

* * *

Ace

I left Cassidy an hour later and walked home. I arrived to find my mother in the kitchen, surprised to see she was still awake. "What are you doing up?" I asked, kissing her cheek.

"Waiting for you," she said.

"Why?"

"Because you're making a mistake and I don't want to watch it happen again."

I braced myself. "And what mistake would that be?"

"You taking up with Cassidy Dennis again."

I frowned as I sat at the island. "Mom, you need to quit with all of this."

"I'm just trying to understand what this new obsession with you is." She crossed her arms and faced me, leaning against the sink. "We never see you... you haven't been home in almost a decade, haven't even been to the beach house in more than two years, and now you're suddenly here?"

"I'm here, Mom, I thought you'd be happy about it."

"I *am* happy about it, honey. What I'm concerned about is you disappearing again. We've seen you twice in the last year and that's because we came to Portland. Before that, it was once in two years."

"I'm not gonna disappear, Mom."

"Forgive me if I don't believe you." She frowned. "She

took you away from me and then Aidan followed because he does whatever you do, including "protecting" the crazy Cassidy Dennis. I can't help but think it'll happen again."

"First of all, she's not crazy, and if you say that again, I'm out of here for good. Second, she didn't take me away from anyone, Mom—"

"She got pregnant with another man's baby, Carter, what would you call it?"

"Be very careful how you proceed, Mom," I warned. "Cassidy was young, and she made a mistake, but I could have easily made the same one and you know it. Regardless of her getting pregnant, though, she's not the reason I left. I left because of my career."

"You left because she broke you."

"Damn it, Mom, I did not!" I snapped.

"Hey, what's goin' on?" Jaxon asked as he walked into the kitchen.

"Nothing, Jax," Mom said.

Jaxon sat next to me at the island. "Where's Dad?"

"Asleep."

"Is that why you're yellin' at Carter?" Jaxon pressed.

"I'm not yelling at anyone."

"Kinda sounds like you're yellin' at Carter."

She jabbed a finger between us. "You two better not gang up on me or we're going to have a problem."

"Mom," I said with a sigh. "No one's gangin' up on you, but you need to hear me on somethin' because I'm not gonna keep goin' around and around on this subject. Cassidy's gonna be part of this family one day... if I had my way, it'd be tomorrow, but she's making me wait and I think it might have something to do with you and your opinion of her. So, you need to fix it. If you don't want to fix it, that's your choice, but you want me in your life, you will love my girl and mean it, because if you don't, I'm gone."

My mother gasped and threw her hands in the air. "See?"

"See what, Mom?" I challenged.

"She's taking you away from me again."

"Fuck me, woman, I can't talk to you right now."

"Don't you dare talk to me that way," she warned.

I took a deep breath. "Mom, I love you. I will always love you, but you're not hearing what I'm telling you. *I* am the reason Cassidy did what she did. This whole fucked up situation is on me and I will do anything to fix it because I love her. I have always loved her. She's it for me and you know it. Whether you choose to believe my reasons for leaving and staying away or not, those reasons have nothing to do with Cassidy, and more to do with me workin' shit out. I'm going to marry her and I'm going to adopt her little boy because in my heart he's mine and he always will be. You either get on board with this and make them both feel loved or we're done." I crossed my arms. "By the way, what happened to the letters I asked you to forward to her?"

"You can't be serious."

"You didn't send them, did you?"

She had the good sense to lower her head.

"And did you send her some email saying I'd met someone and it was serious?"

"I—" She cut herself off, and I knew immediately she'd done it.

"Where are the letters?" I demanded.

"I threw them away."

"Fuck me," I growled. "I'm going for a walk."

I walked out of the house and stamped down my anger. Cassidy was right, and I hated that she was right, more because the thought of her feeling unloved was beyond me. Shit!

I pulled out my cell phone and sent a quick text before heading Cassidy's way.

ELEVEN

Cassidy

I HEARD THE buzz of my cell phone and set my Kindle aside. I couldn't imagine who would be texting me at midnight other than Carter, but we'd just seen each other, so hopefully, something wasn't wrong.

Open your window, babe

I frowned and slid out of bed, pushing open the window and peering into the dark.

"Cass?" Carter whispered.

"I'm here," I whispered back. "What are you doing?"

"Comin' up, give me a sec."

I shook my head and stepped back from the window, forcing down a groan as I watched Carter shimmy his way out onto the large branch closest to my window and swing into my room with a thud. "Fuck me, that's harder than I remember."

I giggled. "Well, you are twice the size you used to be."

"Not quite." He turned and closed the window and then slid off his boots.

"You okay?"

Carter sighed and wrapped his arms around me. "I am now."

I hugged him back. "What happened?"

"Just missed you."

I pulled away and frowned up at him. "Honey, you saw me less than an hour ago. What happened?"

He sighed and dragged his hands down his face. "Nothin' for you to worry about, yeah? Just workin' some shit out and needed to hold you for a bit."

"Translation, your mom's not happy we're seeing each other and giving you grief."

"Babe, it's not your problem."

"It is if you have to choose between us. I can't be the reason you're estranged from your family, honey, and if I lose you... well..." I couldn't even verbalize the thought.

His hand slid to my neck and he pulled me against his chest. "Again, you're not gonna lose me. And if my mother doesn't pull her head out of her ass, any estrangement that might result from that'll be on her. She threw away my letters to you."

"What?" I whispered.

"And sent you the email."

"Why?"

"Who the fuck knows? She's obviously demented. But it doesn't matter, Cass. I love you. She can't come between us anymore."

I hugged him tighter. "So, are you staying here tonight?"

"If you want me to."

"Yeah, I want you to." I smiled up at him. "But the rules still apply."

"I don't have any condoms with me, so I'll keep my clothes on," he promised. "But I'm not promising I won't cop a feel."

I grinned. "I'm counting on it."

The way my parents' house was set up was unique. They'd built it to their specifications and it might be a little weird to some people, but it worked perfectly for us. On both the first and second floor there were bedrooms with attached baths. My parents took the downstairs one and Shannon got the upstairs master since she was the eldest. I didn't mind because my room had the tree.

There were two bedrooms with a jack-and-jill bathroom between, which Mia and I shared. It was a little different since we each had a toilet and a sink, but the shower, bath combo was between the toilets. There were also another two bedrooms with one more bathroom on the second floor which was where all the kids now were. One of them used to be a TV room, but had been converted when we'd all left.

He grinned and slid his hands under the waistband of my panties and cupped my bottom. "Fuck, your ass is incredible."

"You think so?"

"Yeah, baby. Everything about you is." He frowned. "Why?"

I shrugged. "No reason."

He moved his hands to my waist. "You get that you're gorgeous, right?"

I snorted. "Don't be a dork, Carter."

"Baby, look at me."

"Let's just go to bed," I said, and tried to pull away, but he held firm.

"Hey, this is important, Cass." I met his eyes and he smiled. "There isn't a more beautiful woman in the world to me."

"Well, you haven't seen me naked yet."

"So, let's make that happen."

"Soon."

He frowned, but he let me escape and I flipped off my light and slid under the covers. Carter climbed in beside me and pulled me close.

"I love you, Cassidy."

I rolled to face him and stroked his cheek. "I love you, too."

"You on the pill?"

I shook my head. "Not currently, no, but I'll make an appointment with my doctor this week and take care of that."

His hand slid under my cami and cupped a breast. "That'd be good, baby."

I arched into his hand as his thumb slid over my nipple. "Wow. Maybe you should have brought condoms."

He chuckled. "I don't need condoms to take care of you, honey."

"Yeah, but what about you?"

"Tonight's about you." Carter moved his hand from my breast to the apex of my thighs. "No screaming though."

I giggled. "I don't scream, honey. I told you that."

"That's only because no one's ever made you scream." He slipped his hand between my legs, keeping the barrier of my panties between us, and his thumb circled over my clit.

I took in a deep breath. "Possibly."

He grinned and shifted, pushing me onto my back. He sat up and knelt between my legs, shoving the covers off of us and tugging on my panties. "Lift, baby."

I lifted my hips and he slid my underwear off, throwing them to the side. Next came my cami and I was glad it was dark outside... I just wished the moon would hide as well. Although, they say that candlelight and moonlight is romantic and always make people look their best, so I hoped it worked in my favor.

Carter didn't waste any time with words or kisses, he went straight for my clit, sucking gently at first, but increasing the pressure as my body responded. I mewed as he licked, sucked, and blew me into a near climax, stopping just as it built and causing me to cry out, albeit quietly. "Don't stop," I complained.

He chuckled. "I'm not stoppin', baby, just building you up."

"Well, don't do that either." I arched into him. "More."

Carter tugged my hips, so I'd slide further down the bed and guided my legs over his shoulders. "My girl's got a greedy little cunt."

I nodded, and he slid two fingers inside of me while his tongue swirled my clit.

"Ohmigod," I breathed out as his fingers swiped the walls of my vagina. "Yes."

He pressed in again and then began to pump his fingers into me as he sucked on my clit. I felt my orgasm build and then his mouth covered me as I exploded.

"Fuckin' honey, baby," he said as he kissed each thigh and crawled up my body.

"Are you sure you don't have any condoms? Like in your wallet or something?"

He laughed against my neck as he kissed me just below my ear. "Didn't really plan ahead, baby. I can run home and grab them, but I'm not ready to burst our little bubble just yet." He kissed me. "I'm also not done."

"Ohmigod, again?"

"Unless you don't want me to."

I cupped his face. "I absolutely want you to."

He grinned and kissed me again before sliding back down my body and providing me with two more mind-blowing orgasms before I crashed in his arms and didn't wake up again until nature called at around four a.m.

"Babe," Carter whispered as I slid out of bed.

"Gotta pee," I returned. "Go back to sleep."

"Confession? You've kicked me four times, so sleep's not comin' easy."

"Ohmigod, honey, I'm so sorry."

He chuckled. "It's okay, I've got a plan."

"I'll pee and then you can enact your plan."

On my way to the bathroom, I found my discarded clothing, grabbed a pair of clean panties, and made myself a little less naked before stretching out next to Carter again.

"Why'd you get dressed?" he grumbled as he wrapped an arm around my waist and kissed the back of my neck.

I smiled. "In case Maverick decides to wake me... us earlier than usual."

He sighed.

I rolled to face him. "What do you care? You're still fully clothed."

"Yeah, but I like having your naked body close."

I giggled. "You'll have it again."

"Can't wait." He grinned, kissing me quickly. "Pill next week, right?"

"Yes, honey. Promise."

"Can I go back to sleep now?"

"You could have gone back to sleep before," I countered.

"I need to hold you to the bed first."

"You're crazy."

"Roll over, baby."

I did, so my back was to his front and he threw a leg over my thigh and his arm over my waist.

"Mmm, love you, Carter."

"Love you too, baby."

With his arms wrapped tightly around me, I fell asleep within minutes and didn't wake again until I heard the squeal of children's laughter filter in through my open window. I rolled over and found my bed empty, so I sat up and slid off the mattress. Checking my phone, it was past ten, so I peeked outside and grinned. Carter was running around with Maverick and Kai, throwing a football, and my brother-in-law, John was close, holding Alana.

Since my child was in good hands, I showered quickly

110

and then headed downstairs where Mom, Shannon, and Mia were in the kitchen making something that smelled a lot like cinnamon rolls. Dad was sitting at the table, sipping his coffee and reading the paper.

"Why didn't anyone wake me?" I asked as I poured myself a cup of coffee.

"Carter said you should sleep," Shannon offered.

"Are you gonna bust her for having a boy in her room?" Mia asked.

"If it were anyone other than Carter, then probably," Dad said.

I gasped. "You're on the Carter fan committee too?"

"President, honey," he said, and raised his mug in mock toast.

"Why am I just finding all of this out?"

"Because we've been trying not to meddle," Mom said, and kissed my cheek as she passed me to deliver a cinnamon roll to my dad.

I heard the sliding glass door open and turned just as Maverick walked into the kitchen, followed by Carter and John.

"Morning, Mom," Maverick said.

"Hi, kiddo. Having fun?" I asked and hugged John in greeting, taking the baby from him.

"Yeah, I beat Carter at football," Maverick said.

"You did?" I caught Carter's eye and smiled when he shook his head before kissing me quickly.

"He did great," Carter said.

"How about you wash up, Mav, and then you can have one of Grandma's cinnamon rolls."

"Okay!" he said, and headed to the sink.

I slid into Carter's arms and grinned up at him. "You let him win, I take it," I whispered.

He chuckled. "I'll never tell."

"Did you sleep?"

He nodded. "You tried a few times to pull away from

me, but settled quickly. We might need to buy some hand-cuffs or something and lock you to the bed."

I giggled. "Kinky."

"Hell yeah," he whispered, and kissed me.

The rest of the morning was spent getting reacquainted with my niece and nephew, and firmly cementing Carter's place within our family dynamic. Carter had apparently talked with my parents about staying with us for the remainder of the trip, which they quickly agreed to, and Jaxon dropped the dog off before he left (earlier than planned).

"I feel like I've totally screwed everything up," I admitted after we put Maverick to bed that night.

"How so?" Carter asked, pulling me onto the loveseat (and practically in his lap).

"Jaxon left early, you're here... your mom's probably seething right now."

"Who wants wine?" Shannon called from the kitchen.

"Me, please," I said.

"I'll grab a beer in a bit, Shan," Carter returned, and then focused on me again. "You haven't screwed anything up, Cassidy, got it?"

I sighed. "So, why did Jaxon leave early?"

"I have no idea. He said it was a work thing." He smiled. "And I'm here because I love you. Whatever my mom's issues have nothing to do with us."

I bit my lip and studied him for a few seconds. "Okay, I'm dropping it."

He grinned and kissed me. "Thank you. You're it for me, baby. Don't ever doubt it."

"Same, honey."

Carter kissed me again and then rose to get his beer.

"Grab me some cheese when you come back, would you, please?" I called.

"Sure."

The rest of the family filed in as I grabbed a stack of movies and we went through the voting process of which one to watch.

Once the film had been picked, I handed the remote to my dad, and curled up next to Carter again, promptly falling asleep.

I woke the next morning in my bed with his arms wrapped around me, and smiled realizing just how strong he was. I didn't even know he'd moved me.

God, I loved this man.

TWELVE

Cassidy

THE FOLLOWING SATURDAY, I woke up to the sound of Maverick and Carter laughing again. I hadn't seen Carter Wednesday or Thursday, our schedules were too crazy, but he'd come over last night and stayed, and I realized pretty quickly I could seriously get used to this sound every morning. After our incredibly domesticated breakfast, Carter cleared the counter and I loaded the dishwasher while Maverick was washing his face and brushing his teeth.

"Hawk's takin' his boat out in a couple of hours and Payton invited us, along with Booker and Dani. Do you want to go?" Carter asked.

"Hawk has a boat?"

Carter chuckled. "Hawk has a yacht."

"Shut up, really?" I closed the dishwasher and washed

my hands.

He grinned. "Got it real cheap on a repo deal and fixed it up."

"Wow, that sounds fun. I've never been on a boat before."

"Can't wait to see you in a bikini again."

"I don't own one... for obvious reasons."

"What the fu—"

"I'm all clean," Maverick announced as he walked toward us.

"Thanks, honey," I said, sending a warning look to Carter who shrugged. "Carter's invited us out on Lily's dad's boat. How does that sound?"

"Do we get to swim?"

"Yeah, we get to swim," Carter answered.

"Awesome! I'll get my suit."

"You want to pack up whatever you want to take, and we'll swing by my place before we head to the marina?"

"Sounds good. Should we bring food?"

"We'll stop by the store and grab a few things." He grinned. "Your fridge is kind of empty."

I groaned. "I know. I tend to procrastinate on shopping."

"You still hate it, huh?"

"Ohmigod, even worse than before."

He chuckled. "Get your stuff, babe. Jaxon's got the dog, but we'll grab her before we head to the boat."

I nodded and went to find Maverick. "Hey, buddy, you got your suit?"

"Yeah, Mom."

"Good. We should pack a change of clothes and towels as well, okay? Wanna go grab the big towels from the hall closet and bring them to my room, please?"

"Sure."

He scampered off and I took his stuff to my room where I grabbed a canvas tote from my closet and shoved extra clothes inside. I changed into my suit then pulled clothes over the top, and we met Carter in the living room.

"Ready?" he asked.

I nodded. "What about life jackets and stuff?"

"Hawk has all that stuff."

"For Mav too?"

"Babe, he has a daughter, I'm sure he's got plenty of everything."

I cocked my head. "Will you ask him, please?"

With a sigh, he pulled out his phone and sent off a text. "Asked him."

"We'll grab the booster seat while we wait for the answer."

"Are you saying if he doesn't have lifejackets, you won't go?"

I smiled sweetly. "Yes."

He grinned back. "If he doesn't have them, we'll buy them when we go to the store."

"Where are we going to buy lifejackets on a Sunday?"

Carter laughed. "I have no fu—ah... clue."

"Nice save," I said.

He pulled his phone out. "Hawk's got enough lifejackets for sixteen adults and ten kids."

I leaned up and kissed his cheek. "Thank you for asking him."

Carter smiled. "Let's go."

I grabbed my keys and followed my boys out.

* * *

Pulling up to Carter's little bungalow in North Portland, I wasn't surprised by his choice of house. He loved all things historic and was handy in pretty much every area, so I knew he would have chosen something to fix up.

"Mom, I gotta go," Maverick said, grabbing his crotch.

"Let's get you inside, then." Carter helped him out of his booster and we headed up to his house. Opening the door, the dog barked and came running to us. "Hey, girl... I guess

116

Jax dropped you off, huh? Saves me some time." He spent a few seconds greeting Cassidy the dog and then guided Maverick to the bathroom while I took in the living room that we'd walked right into. A fireplace with built-in, glass-front cabinets on each side took up the wall to my right with a modern sofa and two chairs facing it. I wondered if Carter's mom had helped decorate the room, since the painting above it looked like the one that had been in their hallway.

Carter returned, setting a leash and dog bowl on the coffee table. "I have a few things to grab and then we should be set, but do you want a tour first?"

"That would be great," I said

"Can we go now?" Maverick rushed toward us.

I ruffled Maverick's hair. "Carter's gotta get his stuff, so we'll explore for a bit."

"Can I play with the dog?"

"Sure, buddy," Carter said.

"No going outside though," I added.

"I won't, Mom."

Carter made his way to the door, locking it and setting the alarm. "It'll beep if the door's opened, just in case."

I nodded toward the fireplace. "Was that painting in your parents' house?"

"Yeah. Anything girly in this house is from Mom."

I giggled. "That doesn't surprise me."

Before we ended the tour in his bedroom, he showed me the big eat-in kitchen which he'd gutted and redid in a modern but warm and inviting way. There was also a formal dining room, hall bathroom, two other bedrooms that were in various states of disarray, and a full basement with bathroom which was on his to-do list next.

Carter's bedroom was almost a carbon copy of his childhood one, only with a king-sized bed. "You brought your furniture with you?" I asked.

"Yeah. It's still good."

I chuckled. "Sure. We'll go with that."

"When we get married, you can change whatever you like."

I shook my head.

"What?" he asked, all innocence and light as he threw clothes into a duffel.

"I'm not having this argument with you again, buddy. Let's just drop it."

"Okay, baby." He kissed my cheek. "We'll drop it. Ready?"

"Yep."

We gathered up Maverick and the dog and headed back to the truck. The sound of motorcycle pipes had me turning to find Aidan parking in Carter's driveway. He climbed off with a grin and stowed his helmet. "Heard there was a boat party."

Carter chuckled. "You'll have to follow us or ride in the back with the dog."

"I'll follow."

"Maverick, come meet uncle Aidan," I said. "He's Carter's brother."

Introductions were made, and then we headed down to the marina.

* * *

Hawk and Payton's boat was incredible, and I was glad I'd insisted on a bottle of wine with all the other food items we brought. The boat was far too shi-shi to not bring a decent bottle of vino, and since Carter grabbed a case of beer and chips, I grabbed cheese and crackers and the like.

Booker and Dani joined us as well, along with Mack, and Dani's best friend Kim. I had instantly liked Mack when I first met him, and it seemed to irritate Carter, which in turn made it all the more worth it to flirt a little. Booker and Dani had also brought beer and wine, but Dani had the fore-thought to bring fruit and veggies, while Payton had every-thing for a sandwich making bonanza. The men took the kids on deck while us ladies sorted out the food. Cassidy the dog tried to stay where the food source was, but one command from Carter and she followed him outside.

"I always feel like I have to have fancy food when I go out on the boat," Payton admitted. "It's just so... I don't know..."

"Shi-shi?" I offered.

Payton giggled. "Yes, it's totally shi-shi."

"Is Macey going to make it?" Dani asked Payton.

"No. Both she and Dallas have to work." Payton handed me a glass of wine. "Macey's my bestie."

"Ah."

"Okay, I'm ready to get my flirt on," Kim declared.

Dani laughed. "With Mack."

"Or that Knight guy. Holy shit, he's hot."

"And Ace's brother," Dani said.

"Yeah, I kind of figured that," she said.

"So, you and Mack aren't together?" I asked.

Kim giggled. "No. Not my type."

"What do you mean?" Dani argued. "Anything with a penis is your type."

"Oh, you're funny," Kim droned. "The thing with Mack is weird... we just kind of figured out pretty quickly we were going to be friends and neither of us wanted to screw it up by sleeping together. Call it evolving as adults or a prem-onition or something, but we would not be good together. But, man, he's gorgeous and super fun to flirt with."

I grinned. "Yes, he is. But don't tell Carter."

Kim locked her lips. "Sealed, babe."

We filed onto the deck, one hand carrying a drink, the other carrying a tray of food that we set on the table by the railing. A strong arm wrapped around my waist as soft lips kissed my neck. "Mack," I whispered. "Stop."

Carter hissed and gave my bottom a gentle smack.

I giggled and turned in his arms once I'd set my wine down. I sighed with visual pleasure. He'd stripped down to nothing but a pair of swim trunks and he was delicious. "Wow. I didn't think you could get better looking."

His body had always been muscular in a lanky kind of way, but now it was ripped. Channing Tatum kind of ripped, only bigger.

His expression of irritation changed to a smile and he kissed me. "Why are you still wearing your clothes?"

"Because I'm not ready to swim."

"So?"

"So, I'm good." I ran my finger over his side. He'd added several more tattoos since I'd seen him without a shirt. He had the *Dogs of Fire* logo over his heart and an eagle across his ribs. On his left bicep, he had a bolt and a nut with my name woven into the threads. "When did you get this?"

He smiled. "The day after you left."

I gasped. "You did?"

"I didn't want to forget."

"I thought you hated me," I whispered.

He cupped my face. "Oh, baby, I could never hate you. I was hurt and wrecked, and a little willing to run into gunfire, but I didn't hate you."

"Ohmigod, did you really run into gunfire?"

Carter chuckled. "I'm not telling you."

"Can we swim now, Carter? Uncle Aidan's in the water already." Maverick asked, appearing out of nowhere and effectively diverting the subject.

True to his word, Hawk did in fact have enough life jackets for everyone and the kids were strolling the boat, decked out in their safety finery.

"*Please*," I urged.

"Please," Maverick added.

Carter studied me for a few seconds before laying his hand on Maverick's head and smiling down at him. "You bet, buddy."

"I'll get Lily." He turned and started to run, but quickly corrected and slowed to a walk. The rule was no running and

I was proud he remembered.

"If you don't have a suit, babe, I'm sure Payton has something you can borrow."

"I'm wearing a suit," I countered.

"Then why are you bein' all weird?"

"I'm not."

"Cass," he said with a sigh. "You're beautiful, baby, you know that, right?"

"Thank you." I smiled. "It's not about that, at least, it's not *all* about that."

"Then what is it?"

"I don't know… I just haven't been in a bathing suit in a long time, and certainly not in front of all these gorgeous men, not to mention their women. God, did you see Kim? She's like a super model."

He rolled his eyes. "If you find women who need to eat a cookie beautiful."

"What?" I giggled.

"Babe, she's the skeleton of a pretty woman. You, on the other hand, are the whole body."

"Whatever." I felt the heat on my cheeks.

"I'm gonna tell you a secret."

"Oh, yeah?" I craned my head to look up at him.

"I have always loved you and thought your body was hot, but now that you've gained a little weight, I wanna fuck you every three seconds."

I giggled. "Would that even be possible?"

"Can't wait to find out." He kissed my nose. "You had a little preview last weekend, what do you think?"

I shivered. "I think I want a *lot* more."

He grinned. "Tonight, baby."

I bit my lip and nodded. "Okay."

"Ace," Hawk called. "Comin'?"

"Not yet," he whispered and then grinned. "Clothes off, baby," he ordered, and made his way to the side of the boat.

I climbed up onto the top of the boat where Dani, Kim,

and Payton were letting the sun tan them while they watched the rest of the group in the water.

"Hey, Cass," Dani said. "Do you need a suit?"

"No, I'm wearing one."

"Well, get comfy, girl. Soak up some Vitamin D."

I sighed and pulled off my shirt and slid my shorts down my legs. I heard a whistle and followed the sound to find Carter giving me a thumbs-up. He had Maverick on his shoulders and they were horsing around. Cassidy the dog was swimming close to them, her doggie life jacket helping to keep her buoyant.

I gasped when Carter chucked Maverick in the air, but he didn't throw him far, and Maverick squealed with laughter as he bobbed in the water.

"The guys won't let anything happen to Maverick," Payton promised and patted the towel she'd laid out for me next to her. "Come and relax."

I lowered myself and smiled. "I don't even know what that means."

"Well, reacquaint yourself with what we call 'a break,'" Dani said. "You deserve it."

"Twist my arm."

"Do you need lotion?" Dani asked.

"Oh, yeah, that would be great," I said, and took the tube from her. "I put sunblock on my face, but forgot about my pasty white legs."

"I would kill for legs like yours. Mine are more in the vein of tree stumps."

"Danielle Carver, I heard that," Booker bellowed.

"Then quit eavesdropping."

She and I peered over the side to see him just below us.

"Stop insulting my woman," he countered. "Get me?"

She wrinkled her face and mimicked his words with her mouth.

"Dani," he said, his voice low.

"I got you, baby." She smiled down at him. "Love you."

"Love you too. Hawk said there are some water noodles up there somewhere."

"Oh, here," Payton said, and opened a trunk in the corner. "How many do you want?"

"Two's good."

She pulled out two and dropped them down to him.

He gave her a chin lift and swam back to the group. Dani's face got dreamy and I bit back a giggle. For such a sweet, innocent kindergarten teacher, she'd certainly nabbed herself the perfect bad boy.

Finding my own bad boy in the small group of swimmers, I smiled as he helped Maverick and Lily with the water noodles, making sure they were good before letting go. If he hurried up and figured out the correct way to ask me to marry him, we could get on with our lives, but for now, I was engaged in a game of proposal chicken.

"You take Maverick to that Kids' Palace daycare, right?" Payton asked.

"Yeah, it's great. The bus drops him off after school and then I pick him up. Are you looking for something for Lily?"

Payton nodded. "Just a couple times a week when I have a teacher meeting or Alex is working late."

"It's really fun... and cheap." I slathered lotion over my legs. "I'll get you all the info if you like."

"That would be great."

I laid out flat and closed my eyes, the soft musical sound of the ladies' conversation, lulling me into a half-sleep kind of feeling, however, the sudden icy spray of water had me jumping up with a squeal. I noticed I wasn't even close to the towel I'd been sleeping on earlier and had rolled from under the awning that hadn't been there earlier. Classic Cassidy, running even in my sleep.

Carter and Maverick stood in front of me laughing hysterically, the obvious source of my unwelcome shower. "I hate you both."

"Not really, right Mom?" Maverick asked, still trying to

figure out sarcasm from reality.

I smiled. "No, not really."

He grinned. "Lily said her mom and dad brought ice cream. Can I have some, please?"

"Sure buddy, after dinner," I said, noticing that Payton and Dani weren't with me.

"Careful on those stairs," Carter reminded him, and watched him walk down, returning to me a few seconds later.

I jabbed a finger at him. "You I still hate."

He chuckled. "Couldn't resist."

"Hmm-mm." I couldn't help but smile. He was hard to stay mad at.

"Babe, you look a little red."

"I do?"

"Yeah." He frowned. "Why the fuck did they leave you up here exposed?"

"Honey, it was probably me." I glanced down at my body and he was right, my arms and legs were pink. "I'm sure it's fine. It doesn't hurt."

"We'll get some aloe on it in case." He kissed me quickly. "Come downstairs, we're gettin' ready to eat."

I slid on my shorts and T-shirt and followed him downstairs.

"Ohmigod, Cassidy," Dani exclaimed. "You're red. I'm so sorry! We rolled the awning down to keep the sun off, it must have shifted."

"No, I have a sleeping problem," I confessed. "I don't sleep still, so I'm sure I probably rolled out of it. Don't worry about it."

"I should have checked." She frowned. "I'm so sorry."

"Don't even worry about it," I assured her. "Seriously."

"I'll grab you some aloe."

I sighed, and she rushed off to find some.

THIRTEEN

Cassidy

LATER THAT NIGHT, I put Maverick to bed then climbed into the shower, whimpering as the water hit my arms and legs. I turned the tap to lukewarm and grabbed the soap. Holy crap I was burnt to a crisp. I was naturally fair and wasn't a huge sun person, so I couldn't remember a time I'd just laid out like that. Even at the pond, I was in the water more than sunning myself, and my mom would load me up with SPF-4,223.

I shampooed my hair quickly, hissing when I realized the top of my head was burnt as well. I couldn't bring myself to condition even though I knew my curls would cause a mutiny. I would just have to deal with it all later.

Drying myself was just too much, so I gingerly slipped into my robe and woodenly walked down the hall.

"Babe, you okay?" Carter asked.

"No," I grumbled.

Carter followed me into my bedroom, his mouth dropping open. "Holy shit."

I nodded. "Even my hair hurts."

"Baby." He closed the distance between us. "How long were you in the sun?"

"I have no idea. Maybe half an hour. You know what I'm like when I sleep, I probably rolled totally out of cover."

He nodded. "Where's that aloe Payton gave you?"

"In my purse."

"I'll get it." He left me, returning quickly with the tube. "Want to get dressed first?"

I bit my lip. At least my face was okay... I'd slathered it and my neck with SPF50, but neglected my head and the rest of my body. "I can't move my arms."

"Want some help?"

"I guess." I groaned. "So much for our romantic night... we could still try," I joked.

"Sex with lobsters isn't really my thing, Cass," he retorted.

I moved to hit him, but the motion shot pain through my skin and I groaned.

He grinned and kissed me quickly. "Sorry, baby."

Carter helped me into undies and a T-shirt, then gently slathered aloe onto my worst areas. I couldn't bear for him to touch my head, so he left it alone. Needless to say, sleep didn't come easily or stay long that night. We'd snuck the dog into the apartment and she was happy to sleep with Maverick, but I heard her whine at about three that morning and then doors opening and closing, albeit quietly, which meant Carter must have taken her out.

I didn't think I'd fall back to sleep anytime soon, so I headed to the kitchen for some water. Carter walked back into the apartment a few minutes later. "Hey, can't sleep?"

he whispered and set the dog's leash on the counter.

I nodded. "I'm fine as long as I stay on my back, but as soon as I roll it hurts."

Carter gave me a sympathetic smile. "Let's get more aloe on you."

I nodded, and after he put the dog back in with Maverick, I let him slather me with relief.

* * *

We settled into a comfortable routine for a week or so, Carter giving me space because of my sunburn, but waging a sensual war that was quickly breaking down my defenses. The sunburn healed in less than a week, but every time we planned time alone, we were interrupted, and I was sure the universe was against us.

Hawk and Payton had signed Lily up for two days at daycare, and Payton and I had discovered the kids were two peas in a pod... much like Carter and I had been. This fact began the scheduling of many play dates and the blessed option of alone time with Carter.

One such Friday night, Carter had surprised me by taking me into the Pearl for dinner and then back to his place. We'd watched Lily the Friday before and now Payton and Hawk were returning the favor.

Cassidy the dog met us at the door and we kicked off our shoes and spent a little time with her after putting our leftovers in the fridge. Once Carter grabbed himself a beer and poured me a glass of wine, he took my hand and led me down the hall to his bedroom. "How many days have you been on the pill now?"

I tugged on his hand and he turned to face me. "Nine."

"Good, we can forego condoms."

"But..."

"I'm clean, baby." He kissed me then stepped into the bathroom and I heard the shower start. "I got tested and the results came yesterday. Envelope's on the dresser," he called.

He walked back into the bedroom, his chest bare, his jeans unbuttoned. I swallowed my squeak of desire.

"Am I talking over you?"

"A little," I admitted.

"Sorry." Carter smiled and slid his hand to my neck, giving it a gentle squeeze. "I just don't want you to back out."

"I can't back out of something I haven't agreed to."

"What's the hesitation, Cass?" He smiled. "The real one, not the 'we need to wait for Maverick's sake,' or you're burnt to a crisp, 'cause those are kind of moot now."

I wrinkled my nose. "I hate that you know me so well."

"No you don't."

"It's not that I'm hesitating, per se." Unable to stop myself, I ran my fingers across his six-pack. "It's just that this will be my first time since... well..."

"I know."

I dropped my head back to meet his eyes. "I don't know if you do. That night with Pierre was awkward and that's all I really remember. It didn't really hurt, but, well, he wasn't very nice..." I groaned. "I don't really know what I'm trying to say."

"What do you mean he wasn't very nice?"

"He just pointed out things that I needed to work on."

Carter's body locked. "Like what?"

"Nothing, don't worry about it."

"You know if I ever meet this bastard, I'm gonna fuckin' kill him."

"Well, you won't, so it's good. It's not like he didn't have some valid points. We were dancing and ballet is—"

"Fuck me, Cassidy. I swear to *Christ*, if you say one more negative thing about your body, I'm gonna get on a fuckin' plane, hunt that bastard down and beat the shit out of him." He cupped my face. "You. Are. Perfect."

"You haven't seen me naked yet."

"Yes, I have, or did you forget I spent a lot of time exploring you and feasted on your pussy?"

I shivered. "Well…"

"Plus, I put Aloe all over you."

"But that was clinical."

Carter chuckled. "Explain the raging hard-on, then."

"You were hard?"

"Yeah, baby." He sighed. "You didn't notice I took a really long shower?"

I blushed. "I just thought you took long showers."

Carter laughed. "Yeah, not that long, baby."

I swallowed.

"I'm gonna take care of you, honey."

"I know. It's just that my first time was underwhelming and then it never happened again. I guess I don't really know entirely what to expect."

"I do." Carter chuckled. "Babe, trust me. Tonight won't be underwhelming. I promise."

"For me maybe," I grumbled.

"For either of us." He kissed me quickly. "I have never made love to anyone, Cassidy, so I can't wait to find out what that feels like."

"What do you mean? You've slept with more than a few women."

"But I've never made love to any of them. You're the only woman I've ever loved, and I'm gonna prove how much tonight." He cupped my neck. "Trust me?" I nodded, and he kissed me. "I'm gonna shower quickly. Wanna join me?"

I nodded again, and he smiled, taking my hand. Leading me into the bathroom, he slid my shirt over my head and cupped my breasts. "Fuck, babe, seriously, gorgeous." He unhooked my bra and slid it down my arms, cupping me again and drawing each nipple into his mouth. I shivered, the sensation one I hadn't felt before, and he slid his hands under the elastic waistband of my skirt, pushing it down over my hips. I stepped out of it and kicked it away from us. I was so glad I'd shaved my legs that morning. I was also glad I'd worn my one matching set of underwear. A white lace pair of boy shorts and bra. Not that they stayed on my body long.

"Your turn," I breathed and finished unbuttoning his jeans. He pushed them from his hips and then his boxer briefs and his cock stood hard before me. God, it was huge. I know I didn't really have a basis for comparison, but I was a little concerned he might be too big for me. "Um…"

"What's wrong?"

"Are you going to fit?"

Carter laughed. "You're really good for my ego, baby."

"But I'm kind of serious."

"I'll fit, sweetheart. Don't worry." He guided me into the shower and wrapped an arm around my waist, sliding his other hand between my legs. I gasped when his thumb slid over my clit.

"Fuck, baby," he breathed as he slipped two fingers inside of me. "You're so wet."

I giggled. "Should I state the obvious?"

Carter chuckled and stepped under the showerhead, running his hands through his hair before pulling me to him and turning me into the spray. He lathered his hands with shampoo and gently washed then conditioned my curls, then he poured body wash on to a shower poof and ran it over my back.

"Is that my stuff?"

"Yeah, baby. Picked up a few things for you last week for when you're ready to spend the night." He kissed my shoulder. "Got shit for Mav too."

"And the poof?" I couldn't stop a giggle because, let's be honest, 'poof' is kind of a funny word to repeat when you're about to get it on. I kept imagining Barry White with a shower poof.

He raised an eyebrow at my laugh. "The poof is brand new, Cassidy."

"Good answer." I sighed and leaned into his touch.

He chuckled. "Never brought a woman back here, baby."

"Really?"

"Really."

"Another good answer," I whispered as he slid his hand between my legs again.

I braced my hands on his shoulders and wrapped my legs around his waist as he lifted me, anchoring my back to the wall.

"Gonna go slow, baby, but we can stop if you need to."

I nodded, and he lowered me onto him. I let out a deep breath as his girth filled me, his tip feeling as though it was touching my womb.

"Too much?"

I shook my head and leaned down to kiss him. His tongue met mine while his hands gripped my bottom, digging into the flesh that was much softer now than it had been years ago. One arm slid up my back and cupped the base of my skull holding me steady while he began to move. Slowly, giving my body a chance to get used to him. "Carter," I whimpered.

"Need me to slow down?"

"No. God, it's amazing."

The gentleness of his earlier movement changed and he began to thrust deeper, faster, harder, my arms locked around his neck as my body quickened. I felt my orgasm build and slid my hands into his hair, gripping his head as I screamed on my climax.

Carter wasn't far behind me and he dropped his head on my shoulder and we tried to catch our breath.

"Damn, you're strong, baby. I think I love ballet now." I chuckled, and he slid out of me and pulled us both back under the water. He kissed me, running his hands through my hair. "You okay?"

"Yes," I said. "That was… amazing."

"We'll get dried off and do it again."

"You can do it again so soon?" I blushed at his cocky grin. "Of course you can, never mind," I mumbled.

Carter flipped off the water and gently dried my hair before focusing on my body. I let him tend to me, closing my eyes as he did. Before I knew it, I was in his arms and he was carrying me to bed. Pulling down the comforter and sheets, he laid me across the mattress, kneeling between my legs and pushing my knees open. Guiding my legs over his shoulders, he covered my core with his mouth and sucked my clit. I let out a little mew as he continued to lick, suck, and stroke me to near orgasm again. One firmer suck had me breaking and, as I climaxed, he slid into me. I arched against him, his sheer size nearly driving me to climax again. He rolled onto his back, carrying me with him so I was straddling him. I anchored my hands on his chest and shifted so I could draw him deeper inside of me.

"Holy shit!" he hissed.

"You okay?" I asked.

"Fuck, you doin' those kale things?"

"Kale things?"

"Fuck, baby." He grabbed my hips and groaned. "Your pussy's… ahhh…"

I contracted around him. "Kegels, baby, and yes, I do them."

"Cassidy," he whispered, reaching for a breast with one hand while thumbing my clit with the other.

I raised up and then lowered myself again, the sensation of him filling me while his thumb worked my clit was overwhelming.

I lowered again and quickly found myself on my back and yanked gently to the edge of the bed. Carter stood between my legs and drove into me so fast and hard, I came before he was done. I cried out and gripped his wrists, but he broke my hold and spread my legs wider, sliding his hands just below the back of my knees, tipping my hips up a bit, so he could go deeper.

He let out a grunt and then a yell before collapsing on top of me and rolling us on our sides, facing each other, still connected. I felt him still pulsing inside of me, the walls of my vagina squeezing him as we came together.

"Fuck!" he breathed.

"Indeed." I ran a finger over his forehead and down the side of his cheek. "You're illegally pretty, Carter."

"Am I?" He caught my fingertip in his mouth and gave a gentle suck.

I nodded. "I don't know if you're pretty enough to pass as a woman—"

"Well, thank God for small favors." He grinned and kissed me. "I love you."

"I love you, too." I rocked against him, feeling him grow hard again.

He cupped my breast and kissed me. "I wanna have a hundred babies with you."

I giggled, but I was cut off when his thumb stroked my clit again. Facing him, I had room to move and I hooked a leg around his hip and pressed in.

"Your cunt's so fuckin' tight and wet," he breathed out. "God, so good."

I flattened my palms against his chest and closed my eyes as he cupped my breast. He rolled a nipple between his fingers and I dropped my head back in ecstasy.

"I'm gonna move you, honey."

"Huh-uh," I complained.

He grinned and nodded. "You'll like this better, trust me."

"I can't imagine liking anything better than this."

"On all fours, baby," he directed, I did as he said. "Cheek to the mattress."

As I did, he slid into me from behind and I whimpered at the feeling. Ohmigod, it was amazing. One hand ran down the length of my back while the other gripped my thigh. He slid out and in slowly before reaching forward and cupping my breast.

"You okay?" he asked.

"Harder."

"Yeah?"

"Hell, yeah," I encouraged.

Carter slammed into me, holding my thighs steady and then he began to move, surging in and out of me faster and faster. I screamed his name as I came around him, but he wasn't done and he ran a finger over my clit, building me up again.

"Grab a tit, baby, let me see."

I braced on one arm while I kneaded my breast with the other, rolling the nipple between my fingers and panting as another orgasm built.

"I'm close," he rasped.

"Come, honey," I demanded as I exploded again.

I felt him pulse inside of me and then roll us onto our sides, my back to his front, our bodies still connected.

He kissed my shoulder. "You screamed."

"I guess I did, huh?" I giggled and tried to catch my breath. "That was mind-blowing, honey."

"Told you."

I squeezed my eyes shut. "Was it okay for you?"

"Baby, I came four times in less than an hour, yeah, it was fuckin' great."

"You haven't done that before?" I felt his body shake with laughter and slapped his arm. "You *have* done that before?"

"Technically, I can go all night, but, no, I've never come that fast or gotten that hard so fast after."

"Oh." I felt quite smug with that information.

His hand slipped between my legs and he rocked into me. "And now I'm ready again."

He made love to me twice more and then it was time to get dressed and pick Maverick up, but Carter promised more of what he gave me, albeit much more quietly, when we got back to my place. He was lucky I wasn't driving, or we'd have been jailed for speeding.

FOURTEEN

Cassidy

THE FIRST MONDAY back to work after our romantic weekend was tough for me. I wanted to live in the erotic cocoon Carter had built for us over the past few days, but I had a living to make and a child to support, so it was back to the grind for me.

It had been a weird day, one I wasn't entirely sure I should (or could) process. The morning had started with an anonymous box of chocolates left gift-wrapped on my desk, a somewhat inappropriate note, which I knew wouldn't have come from Carter. One, he knew I hated that particular brand of chocolate, and he would have signed the note with "Bolt" or something of that nature... this one was signed, "All my love, your future lover."

Lover? Really? God, it was so gross. Soon after I'd

logged into my computer, I got a few texts from a blocked number that kind of freaked me out a bit, and I knew I was going to have to talk to Carter about it eventually.

The cherry on top of my shitty day, however, was when I walked out of work to find two flat tires and a broken back window. I pulled out my cell phone and called Carter.

"Babe, you okay?"

"Not really," I grumbled.

"Where are you?" He sounded panicked.

"I'm still at work. I'm okay, honey, just a little stranded. I came out to find two flat tires and broken back window." I glanced up at the sky, grateful it was clear and acting like an actual summer day.

"We'll be right there. Stay put."

"Okay. Can you grab my dance bag, please?" I asked. "I'm going to have to go straight from here."

"Sure, babe. Give me fifteen minutes."

"Okay, thanks. Love you."

"Love you too."

We hung up and I dropped my phone into my purse.

"Cassidy?"

I turned to see Tom walking toward me. He really was one of the best-looking men I'd ever met. I didn't fully grasp his hotness on the video conference... he was much better looking in person. His father was British and his mother was Korean, which was a beautiful combination, and since he'd been raised in London, he had the sexiest accent in the world. He'd been helping to implement a few of my suggestions for better workflow and I found him easy to work with, funny, and very kind.

"Hey, Tom."

"You okay?" he asked.

I sighed. "Car trouble, I'm afraid."

"Let me drive you home."

"No, I'm fine. My boyfriend's on his way."

"I didn't realize you were seeing someone," he said,

frowning.

I was a little taken aback by his observation. He was an executive, I was an insurance analyst, we weren't even on the same floor of the building and, other than our professional interaction, we didn't have much to do with each other. I had seen him a few times since he started, but usually in the main kitchen or passing in the hallway when he had a meeting. He'd visited the week after he started, but with the work load, we hadn't been able to have lunch. So, outside of the phone and email conversations, we hadn't really spoken much and certainly not about personal things.

"Yeah, I am," I said.

He stared at me as though he was trying to memorize me. It was a little disconcerting.

"Anyway, Carter's on his way, so I'm all good," I added.

"How about I wait here with you until he gets here?"

"You don't need to do that."

"I'm happy to," he said. "Can't leave a beautiful woman to wait alone."

Well, that was a little inappropriate, professionally speaking. On a personal level, though, it was kind of flattering. Working in a predominantly female department, rumors abounded about Tom, but he had a reputation as being pretty buttoned up and unapproachable. All of this information had come from Janie, who'd helped organize his move from our New York office. I thought it was a little weird that he'd been with the company for less than a month and chose to move from such a big city to Vancouver, Washington of all places, but I never voiced my thoughts. I just listened to the women titter on about him and wonder if he were single, married, or perhaps open to a one-night stand.

None of it really mattered or applied to me since I was never in the market for a man... I had always needed one of those about as much as I did the plague, but then Carter showed up and I was done.

"So, tell me a little about yourself," Tom said. "I know

you have a son."

"I do." I smiled. "He's almost seven and he's awesome."

"And is your boyfriend the father?"

He stepped closer to me and I found myself moving away. I don't know why, but I felt a little weirded out by him. Luckily, I didn't have to answer his probing question when I saw Carter's truck driving towards us. He pulled up behind my car and climbed out. I couldn't help but shiver. Dark jeans, motorcycle boots, tight, white T-shirt, and his cut, he was incredible.

"Hey, babe," he said as he eyed Tom and closed the distance between us.

"Hi, honey." I had planned on keeping things low-key, but Carter had other ideas and pulled me close for a mind-blowing kiss. I blushed and broke our connection, clearing my throat. "Where's Mav?"

"I told him to wait in the truck with the dog."

"Good idea."

Tom reached his hand out and smiled. "I'm Tom Dale."

"Ace." Carter studied him, ignoring his greeting, and Tom lowered his hand.

"I thought you said his name was Carter?" Tom countered.

"It's Ace," Carter said, his voice low in warning.

I watched the two men and it dawned on me they were having a pissing contest of sorts. I rolled my eyes and gave Carter's arm a squeeze. "I only have one spare, so I won't be able to drive anywhere tonight."

"Knight's bringin' a truck, babe. He'll tow it back to the shop."

"You a tow truck guy?" Tom asked.

"No." Carter turned toward him slowly. "Are we holding you up from somethin', man?"

Tom gave him a strange smile. "No, just making sure Cassidy didn't need anything."

"Well, I'm here, so she's good."

Tom nodded and turned to me. "You sure you don't need me to stick around."

I felt Carter's body lock and I shook my head. "No, but thanks anyway."

"Alright, love," Tom said.

"Did you just call my woman 'love'?" Carter demanded.

"It's an English thing," Tom said.

"She's not your fuckin' love, get me?" he demanded.

Tom crossed his arms and smiled. I shivered. Creepy.

"Have a good night," Tom said. *"Love."*

Carter struck so quickly, I didn't see it coming, therefore, had no time to react. Before I knew it, Tom was on the ground, blood spurting from his nose, and still, he grinned like he was demented.

"You ever fuckin' look at her again, I'll kill you," Carter threatened, standing over Tom.

I gasped, reaching for Carter's arm. "Carter."

"Well, aren't you the big man," Tom teased as he stood and brushed himself off, pulling out a handkerchief and holding it to his nose.

Ohmigod, this guy was totally weird.

"Have a lovely weekend, Cassidy." Tom walked away, and I watched in confusion.

I frowned up at Carter. "What the heck was that all about?"

"You watch that asshole, Cassidy, and if he gives you anymore trouble I'll deal with it."

"What's that supposed to mean? I get that he's weird," I conceded, "But did you need to hit him? What if Maverick saw?"

"He didn't," Carter said emphatically.

I sighed and glanced at the truck. Carter was right. There was no way Maverick could have seen. There were too many cars in the way.

"Have you never *met* anyone from England?" I accused. "They say 'love' after everything."

"Babe, trust me. He's interested in you, not to mention, warped in the fuckin' head, and I don't like it."

"You're being ridiculous."

Carter didn't get a chance to argue with me since Aidan arrived with the tow truck.

"You got anything you need in your car?" Carter asked.

"No, I'm good."

"Go get in the truck, then."

I frowned up at him. "Are you mad at me?"

Carter sighed. "No, babe. Just go get in the truck, yeah?"

Aidan climbed out of the truck and took in the car. "You okay, Cass?"

"I'm fine, Aidan."

"Truck, Cass." Carter handed me his keys and made his way to Aidan.

I slid into the driver's seat of Carter's truck and tried to shake off his sudden change in mood. Maverick was bouncing in his seat as I tried to give him a hug. "Hey, honey."

"Hi, Mom. Can I ride in the tow truck?"

"Not tonight." I smiled and stroked the dog's head. "But let me move Carter's truck real quick and then you can watch them hook up my car, okay?"

Maverick gave a little fist pump with his, "Yeah!" and I moved Carter's truck.

* * *

Ace

Knowing that Cassidy (or more accurately, Maverick) wouldn't stay in the truck, I took a second to make a phone call before either of them could hear me.

"Yo, Ace," Booker answered.

"Hey, Booker, I need you to check someone out for me."

"Okay, who?"

I gave Booker everything I knew on this Tom Dale asshole and hung up just as Cassidy and Maverick made their way to me.

"Mav wanted to see the tow truck," Cassidy said. "Who were you talking to?"

"No one," I lied. "Hey, Mav, you want to help hook the car up?"

Maverick looked up at Cassidy. "Can I, Mom, *please?*"

"Of course, honey. Just do what Carter tells you to do, okay?"

Cassidy watched us as Maverick helped Knight and me hook up the car. I knew she was worried about my mood, but I was too busy trying to stuff down the intense desire to kill Tom Dale, that I had no energy to talk shit out with her. She didn't have a fuckin' clue the man was sniffin' where he didn't belong. But I did. And I was gonna make sure the dipshit wasn't an issue.

"We'll get you all sorted tomorrow, Cassidy," Knight said. "And someone'll bring your car back when it's done."

"Thanks a lot, Aidan. I really appreciate it."

Knight hugged her and then took off to the shop.

"Are you going to tell me what's bothering you?" Cassidy asked as I led her and Maverick back to the truck.

"No."

"You are infuriating sometimes."

"Just drop it, babe."

Cassidy scowled, but did as I asked and climbed into the truck after Maverick.

I lifted the dog into the bed, then made my way to the driver's side and drove out of the parking lot. "Do you *have* to dance tonight?"

"Um, yes, I have to dance tonight," Cassidy snapped. "Just drop me off and I'll get Kevin to drive me home."

"No."

"Okay, Tarzan, what do you propose?"

I felt my lips twitch slightly at her irritation. "Mav and I'll drop you off and go find something to eat, then we'll meet you back here."

"Sounds great," she ground out.

"Great."

"Great," she repeated, and I tried not to laugh. God, she was cute when she was pissed.

The dance studio was in downtown Vancouver, so I found a spot with a meter and parked. She kissed Maverick and moved to get out of the truck, but I stopped her. "We'll walk you in."

"You don't need to do that, Carter."

"I want to meet Kevin."

"It's fine," Cassidy pressed. "You can meet him later."

"I'll meet him now." Carter turned off the truck and climbed out, walking around the hood to help her and Maverick out.

She climbed down and frowned up at me. "You're a pain in the butt, you realize that, right?"

I grinned and kissed her quickly. "Yep."

"Come on, Mav," she said. "We'll be quick and then you and Carter can go eat."

"Okay, Mom," he said, and unbuckled himself.

She grabbed her bag and we followed her into the dance studio. I didn't like what I saw. Kevin was a bulk of man, barely an inch shorter than me and almost as muscular. He didn't look like what I assumed a male ballet dancer would look like... he was far more masculine than I had counted on. Fuck!

"Kevin!" Maverick shouted, and ran for the man.

Kevin laughed and grabbed him, throwing him up into the air. "Hey, buddy, how are you?" he asked, and set him on his feet.

"Good. Uncle Carter and me are going to get food."

"That sounds great."

I wrapped an arm possessively around Cassidy, but she pulled away and hugged Kevin. "Hey. Sorry I'm late. I had some car trouble."

"I only beat you by ten minutes," Kevin said. "It's all

143

good."

Cassidy pulled away from Kevin and waved her hand toward me. "Kevin, this is Carter."

Kevin reached his hand out and I took it with a chin lift.

"Well, you boys have fun," Cassidy said, and kissed Maverick.

"Want us to pick you up anything, babe?" I asked.

She gave me a sickeningly sweet smile and shook her head. "No, I'm good, *hon*, thanks."

I raised an eyebrow and leaned down to kiss her, but she gave me her cheek, so I slid my hand to her neck and guided her lips back to mine. "Nice try," I whispered, and covered her mouth with mine.

She pinned her lips shut, so I let her have her hissy fit for the moment, but I made sure she knew we'd finish this later.

"Let's go, Mav," I said, and led him out of the studio.

* * *

Cassidy

"You okay?" Kevin asked as I returned from changing into my dance gear.

"Other than wanting to drop kick my boyfriend into next week, yeah, I'm frickin' fabulous."

Kevin chuckled. "I picked up on some tension there. Want to talk about it?"

"No," I said, and began my stretch. "I mean, he's totally all pissed because he thinks this guy at work is interested in me, so he goes all Tarzan on me and barely says a word! God, he's infuriating!"

Kevin smiled. "We are a simple people, Cass."

"Well, *he* is a Neanderthal."

"The same guy you've talked about pretty much nonstop for, I don't know, years?"

"Bite me, Kevin," I retorted. "You were the one who asked me if I wanted to talk about it."

He laughed again. "You're right. My mistake."

I couldn't help but smile. "Let's just forget about my devastatingly gorgeous but annoying man for the moment and dance, okay?"

"You got it."

Kevin and I got down to the business of ballet, and by the time Carter and Maverick arrived to pick me up; I was feeling a little less irritable. Although, that changed when I caught Carter's expression and he was looking at Kevin like he might maim him.

"You're still shifting your weight, Cass," Kevin instructed. "You'll pitch forward if you don't keep your body centered."

"Sorry," I grumbled and scowled at Carter. I stood in front of Kevin and focused back on the mirror. He held my hands, stretched out to the side and ran one arm down my waist. I kept hold of his fingers as I went up on my toe, went into a spin, and ended with my right leg behind me.

"Better," Kevin said. "Do you feel the difference?"

I nodded.

"Okay, let's try the lift again."

I gave Carter a pointed look and he raised an eyebrow and sat down, stretching his arms across the two chairs beside him. Like he was all Zen and crap. I had a check in my gut that I should have told Kevin no to the lift, but he needed to know it would work with his partner and I needed to keep up on my skills.

However, when he lifted me to his shoulders and I swung down, leaving my crotch essentially in his face, I found myself suddenly ripped from Kevin's arms and transferred to Carter's, causing me to lose my breath with an "Oomph."

"What the fuck are you doin'?" Carter demanded.

Kevin raised his hands in surrender and stepped back because he was a frickin' adult and could control his temper. Carter on the other hand, still had his arm wrapped around my waist like a vice grip and I had to pinch his side (*hard*) to get him to release me.

"God *damn* it, Cassidy," he hissed.

I stomped away from him and over to Kevin. "I'm so sorry, Kevin."

"We can work on this next week, Cass. Don't worry about it."

"You're not fuckin' doin' that again," Carter warned.

"Oh, hell yes we are," I snapped.

"You said fuck is a bad word, Mom," Maverick piped in.

"It is," I reiterated, glaring at Carter. "Uncle Carter is going on time-out as soon as we get home."

"Grandpa would 'tan his hide,'" Maverick mimicked.

"Well, Grandpa's not here, so it's time-out for him," I said, and sat down to remove my ballet slippers. I shoved them in my bag, pulled on my sweats and hoodie and then laced up my sneakers.

I was so mad, I nearly chucked a shoe at Carter, but alas, it wouldn't have done enough damage, so I refrained. I rose to my feet and grabbed my bag. "Let's go."

I took the time to hug Kevin really quickly and apologize again, before leading Carter and Maverick out to the truck.

It was times like these that were glaring reminders that I had no support. I couldn't just drop Maverick off at my parents' place so that I could murder Carter and chop him into garbage bag sized pieces without my child seeing it. It sucked.

We drove home in virtual silence. Even Maverick, who could out talk pretty much anyone, must have figured there was something up and stayed quiet.

Once we pulled into the parking lot of my building, I grabbed my purse and bag and waited for Maverick to unbuckle. "Say goodnight to Carter, honey."

"I'll walk you up," Carter said.

"No, you won't," I countered. "We can talk tomorrow… or never."

"You never want to talk to Carter?" Maverick asked, his

voice concerned.

"It's a figure of speech, honey," I improvised. "And perhaps a little hyperbole."

"What's hyperbole?"

"Drama, little man," Carter said. "Women are all about it."

"Bite me," I snapped.

"You want Carter to bite you?" Maverick asked. "Gross."

"I'm walking you up," Carter continued.

I groaned and began to envision all the ways I could torture the man. We made it upstairs and into my apartment. "Go shower, Maverick, then it's time for bed."

"Okay, Mom."

Without argument (rare for him, but I figured he knew it would not behoove him to squabble with me today), he headed to the shower.

"We gonna talk?" Carter asked.

"No." I slammed my bag onto the sofa.

"I'm thinkin' I'm not leavin' until we do."

"Oh, now you want to talk? What's so special about now, huh?"

"Cass," he said with a sigh.

"What? You've been snappy and dickish, not to mention, pounding your chest ever since you picked me up. I get that Tom's weird, but enough for you to shut me out? Then you *totally* embarrassed me in front of a good friend, which was not okay, Carter." I crossed my arms. "So, no, I don't want to talk about it right now. I want to soak in a tub and go to bed… or maybe soak and then look up the best way to dispose of your body."

"You fuckin' refused to kiss me, Cassidy."

"You shut down long before I refused to kiss you… in front of my friend… in public, *again*. Why do you feel the need to ram your tongue down my throat at every inopportune moment?"

"I'm all for opportune moments as well, baby."

His lips twitched which just pissed me off even more. "Oh, bite me, Carter."

"I won't apologize for not likin' that Tom guy, Cass, but I *am* sorry if I was a dick." He slid his hand to my neck and squeezed gently. "He's off, baby, and I didn't like the way he was lookin' at you."

"He wasn't looking at me!" I snapped and threw my hands in the air. "He was just being nice."

"I'm not arguin' with you about this."

"Oh, okay, then. Drive home safe." I pulled away and headed to the kitchen. "Or not. Whatever."

I'm not really sure how long I stood in the kitchen... I busied myself with opening a bottle of wine and pulling out some leftover mac and cheese that Carter had made the day before... from scratch. In fact, my fridge was full of lots of delicious goodness because he'd gone shopping and filled it, but that didn't make me any less mad at him.

"Babe," Carter said from the doorway. "Can we start over?"

I shrugged, shoving the mac and cheese into the micro-wave. He wrapped an arm around my waist from behind and kissed the back of my neck. "I love you, Cassidy, I really am sorry if I was a dick. I will apologize to Kevin if that will make you feel better."

"You should apologize to him because what you did was wrong, Carter. Not to make me feel better."

"Your pussy was in his fuckin' face, Cass."

"Ohmigod, it was *not*!" I craned my head to look up at him. "There's only one face my pussy's ever been in, thank you very much."

Carter smiled but I could tell he was stuffing a laugh. "I will apologize to your friend."

I nodded. "Good."

"But you can't refuse to kiss me, babe."

"Excuse me?" I elbowed him in the side, not that it did

any good. "I am *not* your chattel, Carter. If I don't want to kiss you, I don't have to kiss you!"

He sighed as the beep of the timer sounded and I tried to pull away, but he held firm.

"I know you're not my chattel, Cassidy."

"Coulda fooled me," I snapped.

"I'm sorry, baby." He turned me to face him and stroked my cheek. "Will you forgive me?"

"Yes. But you're never allowed to come to a dance rehearsal again."

He kissed me quickly and then released me. "Even if I promise—"

"Never again," I interrupted, and pulled out my dinner.

"You gonna let me stay tonight?"

I shrugged and took a bite of cheesy goodness.

"Gotta drive you to work tomorrow, babe. It'll be easier to stay here than drive up in the morning."

I shrugged again.

He grinned and pinned me to the counter. "Also, kinda want your pussy in my face again. It helps me sleep."

I shivered and closed my eyes.

He slid his hands to my hips and kissed my neck. "How about instead of you taking a bath, we'll take a shower together, then I massage all your aches and pains away, eat your pussy, and fuck you 'til you come so hard, you can't stay awake?"

I swallowed and opened my eyes slowly. "Can I eat first?"

Carter laughed. "You eat, I'll get Maverick down, and join you in the shower."

I nodded, and he rubbed my arms and kissed my forehead. "I love you, baby."

"I love you, too… sometimes," I grumbled.

"Are you guys gonna kiss?" Maverick asked from the doorway.

I giggled. "Maybe."

"Gross."

Carter grinned. "Come on, Mav, let's get you to bed. Mom needs to eat."

They left me, and I downed my food as fast as I could, grabbed the wine and a glass, and headed to my room. Before jumping in the shower, however, I said goodnight to Maverick and made sure he wasn't concerned about my argument with Carter. All was good in the world of Maverick, so I led Carter to the bathroom.

FIFTEEN

Cassidy

OVER THE NEXT few weeks, Carter became a pretty solid fixture at my apartment, as did the dog. I was half expecting a neighbor to rat me out and contact the management, but so far so good. For the most part, we spent weekends at Carter's place and weekdays at mine, which worked for now, but would probably have to change relatively quickly.

Most weeks, instead of taking Maverick to daycare, Carter would take him to his place on Friday mornings and hang with him while I went to work, and I'd drive to his place in the evening. Maverick loved his one-on-one time with Carter and I loved that I got to sleep in.

One Thursday morning, I got a phone call from the director of the daycare and it seriously put a wrench in my busy day.

"Ms. Dennis, would you please come down? Ah, we need to discuss your son."

My stomach dropped. "Um, sure, is everything okay?"

"We've had an incident, and I think it would be a good idea if we talk about it in person."

"I'll be there as soon as I can." I hung up, let my boss know there was an emergency, and headed to my car. My mind ran rampant with all the issues it could be.

"Cassidy?" I turned to find Tom following me into the elevator. "Everything okay?"

"Something's happened at my son's daycare," I said, and pressed the button to the lobby.

"Can I drive you? You look upset."

"No, I'm okay. I just need to get there as soon as I can."

"Let me drive you," Tom insisted.

"No, it's really okay. Thank you, though." I left Tom standing in the elevator and rushed for my car. I probably broke a few speeding laws, but figured if I got pulled over, the cop would more than likely be sympathetic. I pulled into the parking lot and saw two Harleys parked by the entrance. I recognized Carter's and frowned. I couldn't imagine the school would have called him, unless they couldn't get a hold of me.

Walking into the building, I saw Maverick sitting next to Lily on a chair outside of the director's office. Carter was standing close by.

"Mom!" Maverick called, and rushed to me.

"Hey, honey. You okay?"

"Ms. Dennis, if you could join us, please?" Monica leaned out of her office and waved me in.

I nodded and led Maverick back to his seat. "Just hang for a bit with Lily, okay?"

"Yeah, Mom. I'm protectin' her."

Oh, this did *not* sound good. I frowned up at Carter and then walked into Monica's office and frowned, Carter fol-

152

lowing. Hawk stood looking very fierce and somewhat pissed off, while Payton sat on one of the chairs looking more worried about the state of her husband than anything.

"What's going on?" I asked.

"Have a seat," Monica said. "We've had a little bit of an incident with Maverick and Lily. I must ask your friend to step outside."

"I'm not goin' anywhere," Carter said.

"He's Maverick's father," I said, unsure exactly what to say.

"Oh, in that case, come in," Monica said, and sat at the desk. "Maverick hit another little boy today."

I gasped. "What?"

"Yes. Ethan Walker. According to Maverick, he was harassing Lily and Maverick was protecting her."

I forced myself not to let out a holler of victory.

"Lily, as you know, Mr. and Mrs. James, unfortunately, has a nasty bruise on her arm, and since we have a zero-tolerance policy, Ethan is expelled, however, I'm attempting to figure out the best course of action for Maverick."

Hawk looked like he was ready to kill someone.

"I don't understand," I said.

Monica sighed. "I can't condone violence, Ms. Dennis. Maverick hit Ethan and then put him in a chokehold that caused him to pass out for a few seconds. This is very serious."

"Yes, very serious. I agree," I said.

"Maverick said the reason he put Ethan in a chokehold, was that even after Ethan was hit, he would not release Lily, which I believe is why Maverick went that route... how he even learned how to do that is disturbing, but in this case, it was effective."

I narrowed my eyes up at Carter who gave me a look of complete innocence. Well, right there was proof of how Maverick knew how to do that. Crap!

"So," Monica continued, "I think it would be a good idea

if Maverick takes the week to talk about non-violent ways to resolve his conflict—"

"That little bastard put his hands on my daughter," Hawk said, his tone frightening.

"I'm aware of that, Mr. James."

"He nearly broke her arm."

"I... I know. I apologize..."

"Are you hearing me, lady? He nearly broke my daughter's fuckin' arm. If Maverick hadn't stopped him, he would have. Where the *fuck* were the adults in this fuckin' situation?" he bellowed.

"Honey," Payton whispered.

A disturbance outside had Carter pulling open the door, then, "What the fuck?"

We rushed out to see Maverick shoving Ethan away from Lily, a large man drawing his arm back as though to hit him. Carter moved with lightning speed, as did Hawk. The man I assumed was Ethan's father seemed rather surprised when Carter's fist landed squarely in his face, while Hawk pulled Ethan away, and Maverick rushed to stand in front of Lily, blocking her from harm. I wasn't sure I was correctly processing everything that was happening.

"Ohmigod," Payton said, groaning.

Payton and I guided the children into Monica's office, while Monica pulled Ethan aside. Hawk, Carter, and Ethan's dad had disappeared, but I caught movement out a side window, so I assumed they were having a discussion... well, or something.

"I'm calling the police," Monica stated, and pulled out her cell phone.

"I think we should get the kids home," I said, and grabbed Maverick's hand.

"Good idea," Payton agreed.

"You need to wait for the police," Monica said.

"My husband can deal with the police," Payton said. "I would rather get my daughter somewhere safe... it's obviously not here."

"Yes, what she said," I said, and tugged Maverick toward the exit.

I was pulled up a little as I realized Maverick had taken Lily's hand and was guiding her with us. I caught Payton's eye and she bit her lip... yes, even in the stress of a biker fight, my kid protecting this little girl was adorable.

We arrived at the car, luckily parked in the opposite direction of where I assumed our men were, and I pulled open the door.

"Hold on, Mom," Maverick said, and faced Lily, laying his hands on her upper arms (the way Carter did to me, I might add). "Hey, you okay?"

"I'm okay, Mav," she said, her tiny little voice lilting as she smiled at him with hero worship. "Thanks for helping me."

He kissed her forehead and gave her a hug and I had to turn away and bite my knuckle to keep from sighing out loud. Payton had her lips pressed in a thin line in an effort to do the same.

"I'm gonna make sure Lily gets in her car seat safe, 'k, Mom?"

I smiled at Payton and then turned to the kids. "Absolutely, buddy."

He took Lily's hand and then stared up at Payton. "We're ready, Mrs. James."

"Right," she said, recovering a little slower than Maverick expected. "Let's go."

Payton hadn't parked far from us, so I followed her to the car, sandwiching the kids between us. Once Lily was in the car, she smiled over at me. "Why don't you guys come back to our place for a bit? I don't know how long the guys will be and maybe we can order pizzas or something."

"I feel like we should wait for the police," I said.

"Don't worry about it. Alex will take care of it and if there are any issues, my brother will help."

"Is your brother a cop?"

"FBI."

"Oh, wow."

Payton smiled. "I really want to get Lily home and get ice on her arm. Macey's coming over later, so I'm going to have her look at it."

"Should she go to the emergency room?" I asked.

"No, nothing feels broken. She has full range of motion, so we'll ice and see what Mace says when she comes over."

"Can we go to their house, Mom, please?" Maverick begged.

"Sure, buddy. I'll just text Carter and let him know what we're doing."

"Don't," Payton said. "It'll distract him."

"Good point." I laid my hand on Maverick's head. "Okay, buddy, let's get in the car. We'll follow Mrs. James home."

Maverick buckled himself in and we followed Payton home. I didn't see Carter as we drove out of the parking lot, I did still see his bike, but wondered where the heck the men had gone. We passed a lit-up police cruiser on our way home and my heart raced a little. I'd never been in trouble with the law... or anyone for that matter, so it made me nervous.

We pulled up to a lovely and spacious house in Felida, an upper-class area of Vancouver. It was a newer development and it made me long for a place of our own. Me, Maverick, *and* Carter. I smiled, realizing that it was very, very likely that we'd have it one day.

Maverick unbuckled himself and rushed to open the door for Lily. I caught Payton's eye and we both stifled giggles. Grabbing my purse, I followed her inside the house and, after a quick tour, we sat at the dinette table with the kids while Payton iced Lily's arm.

Hawk and Carter got home less than an hour after us.

I studied Carter's body, checking for injury, but he looked fine... well, other than the knuckles on his right hand.

"Babe, I'm fine," he said, stroking my cheek.

"How bad?"

He studied his hand. "Not bad."

I let out a frustrated snort. "Not *you*, Carter. Ethan's dad."

"Babe, don't ask questions you don't want answers to."

"I'm not."

Carter sighed. "He won't be an issue."

"Did the police come?"

"Yeah, but it's sorted."

"Carter."

"I'm hungry. Are we ordering pizza or what?"

"Honey, seriously, tell me."

He smiled, kissing me quickly. "Ethan's dad didn't press charges, and we didn't either, considering his kid hurt Lily, so it's done."

"Except we need to find another daycare."

"We've got time, Cass. I'll take Mav with me to the shop on days I have to go in and when we get married, we can find a more permanent situation."

I huffed and stalked into the kitchen.

"Babe?" Carter called, following me.

"You okay?" Payton asked me, glancing up from her laptop on the island.

I nodded. "Yep."

"What do you want on your pizza?" Payton asked.

"I like combo, Carter's a ham and pineapple guy, and Mav's all about the cheese."

"Perfect. Ordered." Payton grinned and closed the laptop. "Should be here in half-an-hour or so."

"Don't like ham and pineapple anymore, Cassidy," Carter said.

"Don't care, Carter," I retorted, and sat at the island.

I saw Payton smile and I glared up at Carter, catching his grin before he schooled his features. "What?"

"What?" he repeated, innocently.

"Bite me, butthead."

He leaned down and gently nipped the back of my neck. "Anytime, baby."

"You're an idiot."

Carter laughed. "God, how I have missed that from you."

"Bet you have."

"I still love ham and pineapple."

I rolled my eyes. "Tell me something I don't know, Carter."

"Yoohoo!" a voice called out from the foyer.

"Kitchen, Mace," Payton responded.

"I'll get Lily," Hawk said, and bellowed for her up the stairs.

"Helpful, babe, thanks," Payton grumbled.

Hawk grinned, and Lily and Maverick came down the stairs a few seconds later, Maverick in full protection mode. I was beginning to see that I'd need to have a conversation with him about the difference of being protective and stalker-like.

"Auntie Macey," Lily squeaked and hugged her.

Macey hunkered down in front of her and grinned. "Hey, baby. Mommy said you got a bruise on your arm. I'm gonna look at it okay?"

"Okay," Lily said.

"Mav, let's give them some space," I said.

He frowned and it took him a few seconds before he stepped away from Lily and over to me. I gave Carter a look of frustration and he smiled.

"Hey, Mav, let's go talk for a bit," Carter said.

"I want to make sure Lily's okay," Maverick countered.

"She's okay, bud, but Macey needs to look at her to make sure." Carter laid a hand on his shoulder. "And she needs to do it without us hovering."

Maverick sighed, but followed Carter into the family room. I heard my phone peal from the kitchen and rummaged through my purse to answer it. I didn't recognize the number. "Hello?"

"Cassidy?"

"Yes, this is she."

"Hey, it's Tom."

I frowned. "Oh, hi."

"I'm ringing to see if everything's okay with your son."

"Oh, yes. It's fine. Thank you. How did you get my number?"

"Janie provided it. I hope I'm not overstepping. I was concerned about you and wanted to make sure you were okay."

"Thank you. Yes, everything's fine."

"I'm so glad," he said. "Well, should you need anything, please let me know."

"Okay. Thank you."

"Cheers." He hung up.

"Who was that?" Carter asked as he walked into the kitchen and grabbed a beer.

I shoved my phone back in my purse. "No one."

"Does this no one have a name?"

"It was a telemarketer," I lied. "I didn't ask his name."

"Want a beer?"

I shook my head. "I'm good with pop."

He smiled and wrapped an arm around my waist. "Stop worrying."

I dropped my head to his chest. "Don't tell me what to do."

Carter chuckled, setting his beer on the island and sliding his hand to my neck. "I've got Mav, honey. We'll hang out this week at the shop. He's old enough to hold a wrench and learn how to fix an engine anyway."

I raised my head and bit my lip. "You won't let a car fall on him, or let him fall down into a hole or anything, will you?"

"Babe."

159

"What?" I challenged. "He's a little boy and he's curious about everything, but common sense is not his strong suit."

"I remember, honey. Don't worry, I got this."

I squeezed his middle. "I love you, even if you drive me nuts."

"So, how about we go get married next week?"

"You are *not* going to get a rise out of me, Carter Quinn."

He chuckled again and raised my head for a heart stopping kiss. "We'll continue this later."

I smiled. "We better."

"Come on, let's go join everyone."

"Okay, but I can't make it a late night."

"It won't be," Carter promised. "I need time to do things to you."

I giggled. "You are so romantic."

* * *

Ace

"I'll just grab my beer, babe," I said, and waited until Cassidy was out of sight. I then found her phone, referenced the phone number that had last called her, and put the phone back in her purse. Grabbing a soda for her, I took my beer and followed her into the other room.

Telemarketer, my ass. I knew she lied to me, I just wasn't sure why, but I fully intended to find out.

SIXTEEN

Cassidy

ARRIVED AT the office the next morning to find flowers at my desk. Red roses. Not my favorite, but still, I wondered who would have sent them. Carter wasn't much of a flowers and romance kind of guy… unless he was trying to butter up my mother, plus, he knew sunflowers were my favorite, so he'd never send roses.

"Who are they from?" Janie asked excitedly from my cube door.

I faced her and shrugged, dropping my purse into my drawer. "I have no idea."

"Well, what does the card say?"

I smiled. "You know something, don't you?"

The pretty brunette pressed her lips into a thin line. "I plead the fifth."

I powered up my computer and then opened the card.

"Ohmigod, they're from Tom."

Janie gasped and then gave a girlish giggle. "That's so cool, Cass. He's unbelievably hot."

I groaned. "But he knows I'm taken, Janie. It's a little weird, don't you think?"

"Lady, you're not married. You're not even engaged, so live a little." She leaned against the desk. "Tom is super-hot, super rich, and super interested in you. This guy you're dating isn't even on the same playing field as him. Go for it."

"You know nothing about my boyfriend, Janie, I'd be careful about what you say next."

She raised her hands in surrender. "Not trying to start a fight, Cassidy. It's just that Tom's a catch and you rarely talk about your boyfriend. I saw him when he came to pick you up and he kind of looks rough, you know? Tom's a total gentleman."

"Okay, since I don't really want to get into a cat fight, Janie, I'm going to ask that we stop this conversation. I purposely try to keep my private life private, but I will say something and I need you to hear me. I love my boyfriend. More than you or anyone could ever imagine. Not only is he good to me and my son, and loves us both dearly, he served this country and continues to serve it, so in my eyes he's a hero. Maybe you and other people don't see him on the same playing field as a man like Tom Dale. Well, I'd agree with you there, because Carter is the greatest human being I've ever known, and that includes the great Tom Dale."

"I didn't mean to offend you," Janie grumbled. "I'll talk to you later."

I didn't respond as she walked away from my desk. There was no reason to. Janie Styles was a notorious gossip and could be vindictive as hell. I wasn't interested in getting further on her bad side.

I decided there was only one thing to do. I had to return the flowers to Tom. I grabbed the vase and headed to the elevator. Once at his floor, I squared my shoulders, walked past the executive level receptionist desk, down the hall to his office. I knocked on the door, entered when bid, and set the flowers on his desk.

"You got them," Tom said, rising to his feet with a smile.

"I did. They're beautiful, but I'm sorry, I can't accept them."

"They're just flowers, Cassidy," he argued. "I know you had a rough day yesterday and I wanted to cheer you up."

Well, that was seriously thoughtful.

"That's very kind of you, Tom, seriously, and I don't want to look ungrateful—"

"Then take the flowers back to your desk, Cassidy."

"I can't. I'm sorry."

"You can, love." He crossed his arms and leaned against his desk. "Tell people your boyfriend sent them. It can be our little secret."

"I don't think that would be a good idea." I smiled. "I should get back to my desk. Have a lovely day."

"Have lunch with me," he said to my retreating back.

I faced him again and shook my head. "I brought my lunch today, but thanks for the offer. I really should get back to work."

"No worries," he said, and I hightailed it back to my cubicle.

At just before noon, I entered the main kitchen and opened the fridge. I couldn't stop a little swear as I shoved things around in the icebox. My lunch had disappeared.

"What's wrong?" Janie asked, and grabbed a Coke from the vending machine.

"My lunch has suddenly walked away," I complained.

"Ugh, people suck. Mine got stolen last week. I'm thinking next time I bring something with me, I'm going to put a powerful laxative in it."

"That's actually a really good idea," I said.

163

"Hello, ladies," Tom said, and walked into the room.

"Hi, Tom," Janie said. I just smiled.

"Did you finish up with the board?" Janie asked.

"I did." Tom checked his watch. "Thought I'd grab lunch."

Janie nodded. "You might want to take Cassidy with you. Someone stole hers."

"No, it's okay," I rushed to say. "I've got stuff at my desk."

Week-old Ritz crackers and oatmeal, but beggars can't be choosers.

"Who would steal someone's lunch?" Tom asked, disgusted.

"It happens all the time around here," Janie informed him.

I gaped at her. She was just a *wealth* of information today.

"What do you say, Cassidy?" Tom asked. "Can I take you to lunch? It'll have to be quick because I have a meeting in two hours."

That was a quick lunch? Good lord, to be an executive.

"No, really, it's okay," I said.

"I insist. You've got to eat, after all, and I'm starving." He smiled. "We'll just head to the deli across the street."

I *was* hungry and it was just lunch. Besides, since the deli was within walking distance, it's not like I was getting in a car with him, so it's not like it was a date or anything.

"Okay, sure. That sounds great," I said.

Gah! Why did I feel like I was cheating?

"Shall we?" he asked.

"I'll just grab my purse."

"No, it's on me. We won't be long."

"You kids have fun," Janie said, and I followed Tom to the elevators.

* * *

Ace

I slid out from under the sixty-seven Mustang I was working on and smiled at Maverick who was sitting relatively quietly on a chair by one of the tool cabinets. His face was focused on my iPad, probably because I'd loaded a bunch of games on there for him.

"Ace," Booker called, his voice echoing through the shop.

"Here, brother." I rose to my feet and wiped my hands on a rag... not that it helped much. I probably should have worn gloves, but what I was doing was delicate and I needed to feel my way with limited visibility.

"Got somethin' on that number you sent me."

"Mav, let's go hang inside for a bit," I said, and waited for him to follow me.

Once Maverick was settled safe within sight, but out of earshot, I took the pages that Booker handed me. "The fucker called Cassidy on her cell phone?"

"Yeah. I did more digging and Tom Dale has more than one cell. He has a company one and a private one. He called her from his private one." Booker pointed to page two. "The guy left New York under suspicious circumstances, but nothing's in writing and no one's talking. Mack's got a P.I. looking into it in person. For someone who's made it so far up the chain so young, there's no chatter about him. Not one fuckin' thing, and that doesn't sit well with me. There's nothing positive *or* negative about him."

I skimmed through the information. "Yeah, you'd think he'd have a hell of a lot more out there than this. It reads like a scripted professional biography. Even his social media seems vague."

"Any clue on what he wants with Cassidy?"

"He wants *her*," I said. "But she thinks he's a nice guy with no ulterior motives."

165

Booker sighed. "And she's not listenin' to your warnings."

"Nope. Fuck me, this guy's not right."

"Got your back, brother."

"'Preciate it, Book."

I grabbed Maverick and we headed back into the shop to work on the car some more. I tried to put the pit in my gut aside, but the more I thought about the asshole sniffin' after Cassidy, the more concerned I became.

* * *

Cassidy

Lunch with Tom was surprisingly relaxed and, dare I say, kind of fun. He was funny and sweet, and as Janie had said, a gentleman. He paid for the meal, which I appreciated since I hadn't budgeted for a lunch out that week. I quite liked the man, although, maybe not the same way he seemed to like me.

I was willing to admit that Carter might have been right, but I was confident I could handle the situation... and do it without Carter's Neanderthal interference.

I saw Tom again as I was leaving, but just a wave goodbye, then I was on my way home. I was feeling pretty confident in myself as I walked into my apartment. Even if I wasn't interested in Tom, it was flattering to have such a successful and good-looking man interested in *me*.

"Hey, babe," Carter called from the kitchen.

"Hi, honey." I dropped my purse on the sofa and made my way to him, raising up on tiptoes to kiss him. "How was your day?"

"Good. Yours?"

I smiled. "Well, other than someone stealing my lunch from the fridge, it was good."

"Hi, Mom!" Maverick said, as he wrapped his arms around my waist. "I helped Carter fix a Mustang."

"You did? That's awesome, buddy. What else did you guys do?"

"We ate lunch with the brothers. They were so cool, Mom! But they kind of swear a lot."

I wrinkled my nose. "Well, that's what some adults do, honey, but they're allowed to because they're adults. As long as you don't start copying them, it's all good."

"I won't, Mom." He lowered his voice. "But just so you know, when I make Lily my old lady, I might say 'fuck.'"

"Maverick!"

"Sorry, Mom."

I bit the inside of my cheek to keep from laughing... or washing his mouth out with soap. I was conflicted on which way to go, so I dropped my shaking head onto Carter's arm.

"Go wash up, Mav. Dinner's almost ready," Carter said.

He rushed off to do what he was told, and I dissolved into giggles while Carter wrapped an arm around me. "What are you men teaching my child?"

Carter chuckled. "You'd be surprised by how little they actually swear around him. They're used to watching their tongues with the other kids, but sometimes shit filters out."

"I was wondering more about the whole "old lady" thing. Good lord, are you creating a pint-sized biker badass under my nose?"

He grinned and took a swig of beer. "He's gonna see it with us, so he's gonna have to figure out which way to go when he's older."

"Hmm-mm," I grumbled.

"Did you figure out who stole your lunch?"

I shook my head. "No. I ended up having lunch with..." My plans to filter had just gone horribly wrong, so I grabbed a soda out of the fridge and opened it.

Carter crossed his arms and leaned against the counter. "You ended up having lunch with...?"

I sighed. "You can't get mad."

"Fuck me," he ground out. "You had lunch with that dipshit Tom guy?"

"It's not like it was planned. He was in the kitchen and Janie told him someone stole my lunch. He was being nice!"

"He was probably the one who fuckin' stole it, Cassidy!"

I gasped. "He *wouldn't.*"

"And you're fuckin' naïve if you really believe that."

"Don't talk to me like I'm an idiot, Carter."

"Babe, I don't think you're an idiot. Far from it. And I know why he'd do something like that. If I were him, I'd probably do the same thing."

"You'd steal my lunch," I countered.

"To get you to go out with me? Hell, yeah I would. But it's not just about that." Carter dragged his hands down his face. "What the hell is this fucker up to?"

"Nothing. He knows about you. He knows I'm not interested in him. I've been very clear and you hit him for Pete's sake! Pretty sure he got the picture."

"Guys like that don't listen, Cassidy."

"Guys like you," I observed

"He and I are *nothing* alike."

I rolled my eyes. "I think you and he are more similar than you'd like to admit. You're both strong, successful men, who know what they want and go after it. I certainly never had a chance with you, and can you honestly say that if I decided you and I were over, you wouldn't wage an all out war to get me back?"

"Is that what you want? Us to be over?" His tone was one of anger and panic.

"No! Of course not. I love you. I'm not going anywhere. I'm just simply trying to get you to see it from another side." I slid my hands up his chest and looped them behind his neck. "I think I can handle a man who isn't nearly as sexy and delicious as you are. I think I kind of already have."

"What do you mean?"

"Okay, don't get mad."

"Don't fuckin' tell me not to get mad, Cassidy."

I frowned. "Well, then I'm not going to tell you."

"Mom!" Maverick called. "I'm wet."

"Cassidy," Carter growled.

"We'll talk about it later," I said, and headed to the bathroom. Maverick had managed to soak the entire front of himself while washing his hands. "Oh my gosh, buddy, what happened?"

He lowered his eyes.

"Maverick Carter Dennis, what did you do?"

"I'm sorry, Mom, I just wanted to see how far the water would shoot."

I groaned and grabbed a towel from the towel rack. "Strip."

He removed his clothes and I wrapped the towel around him. "Now, go get in your pajamas, we can skip a shower tonight."

"Yes," he hissed, and jogged off to his room.

"You okay?" Carter stood in the doorway and frowned.

"Yes," I said with a sigh. "Our kid just decided to have a water gun fight without an actual water gun... or a target."

Carter grinned from ear-to-ear as he grabbed another towel and began to help me sop up the water.

"What?" I asked as I stood.

"You just said, 'our kid.'"

I smiled. "Did I?"

"Yeah, baby, you did."

"Well, he is, right?"

"Damn right he is," Carter said, and kissed me. "I love you, you know that, right?"

"Yes. I love you too."

We finished cleaning up the mess and then sat down to eat.

"Maverick, next time you make a mess like that, you'll need to clean it up, got it?" Carter said.

Maverick dropped his eyes to his lap. "Okay."

"And no using language like that, even if you're making

a joke, yeah? At least, not around your mom."

"Not around anybody," I countered.

Maverick gave Carter a little grin, but nodded when I narrowed my eyes at him.

"Okay," Maverick said.

"Apologize to your mom, please," Carter added.

"Sorry, Mom."

I smiled. "I forgive you, buddy."

Carter rustled his hair and we dug into the food. Again, Carter outdid himself with the chili he'd started that morning in the crock pot. I admitted that if he was willing to shop and cook for us, I'd do dishes and laundry, and he'd never hear me complain. The deal was struck and the roses confession was forgotten.

SEVENTEEN

Cassidy

WEDNESDAYS WERE TYPICALLY my night to cook or grab take-out since the club attended "church." You can probably guess that several local fast-food joints had a slight pick-up in business on my nights to cook, but this week Carter made more of his crack-n-cheese as I'd dubbed it. Seriously, I was going to gain a million pounds if I didn't watch it. Of course, I thought all of this while shoveling my third helping of said crack into my mouth.

Maverick was in the shower and I was opening a bottle of wine when my cell phone rang. Assuming it was Carter, I answered it. It wasn't him.

"Hi, Cassidy, how are you?" Tom asked.

"Um, I'm good. How are you?"

"Excellent. I'm just waiting at the airport. Heading to London for the week, then Paris the following week."

"Oh, that's nice." I frowned and shook my head, totally unclear as to why I needed to know this. "Sorry, Tom, this isn't really a good time for me."

"Oh, right. Sorry, love. You're probably getting your son ready for bed."

"Well, have a nice trip."

"'Bye, sweetheart."

I hung up and groaned. Crap! This was getting out of hand. Monday, I'd found more flowers on my desk, which I promptly returned. I was glad he wasn't in his office at the time. Yesterday he'd stopped by my desk to say hello and see how I was, again trying to convince me to keep the flowers.

Today I hadn't seen him, so I had hoped he'd gotten the message, but apparently not. I was not looking forward to the conversation I was going to have with Carter. I knew I needed to tell him everything, but I also knew he was going to overreact.

Once Maverick was in bed, I sat down in front of the television with a glass of wine (and, yes, more crack-n-cheese, don't judge me). I heard the key in the lock an hour later and my man walked in looking hotter than normal in his tight black T-shirt, cut, and jeans.

"Hey, baby," he said, and leaned down to kiss me.

I smiled. "Hi. How was church?"

"Busy," he said, and flopped down next to me. "A lot of shit to cover."

"Good stuff?" He shook his head and I sighed. "Right. Club business."

He smiled. "Yeah."

"Want me to heat up some crack and get you a beer?"

He chuckled. "That'd be great, babe, thanks."

I headed to the kitchen and grabbed everything.

"How was your day?" Carter asked. I didn't answer right away, not entirely sure where to start. "Babe?"

"I have to talk to you about something," I said, as I

walked back into the living room and set his dinner in front of him.

He frowned up at me. "Okay."

"I think I've made an already weird situation worse."

"Honey, sit down and talk to me. Can't fix it if you don't tell me."

"I don't *want* you to fix it, Carter. I just think you should have full disclosure." I sat beside him, crossing my legs in front of me.

"Tell me."

I sighed. "Tom's not really taking 'no' for an answer."

"How so?" he said carefully, and set his beer back on the coffee table.

Uh-oh.

I swallowed. "Well…"

I filled him in on the flowers, the phone calls, the office visits, everything, and found myself scooting back at the rage pouring off of him. Without comment, he knifed off the sofa and grabbed his phone, leaving the apartment, his food sitting untouched on the table.

* * *

Ace

"Yo, Ace," Booker answered.

I sat in my truck, the only place I could get complete privacy. "The fucker's messin' with her. He called her again today… I thought you blocked her number."

"I did. We've been watching his phone. Hold on, let me see if there's anything new."

Booker did whatever the fuck Booker did, and I forced down my desire to break something. Booker could find anyone anywhere and no one questioned if his information came legally or not. He was the club's computer guy and had a knack for hacking pretty much any system, so I had to trust that he'd be able to figure out (at least on the cyber side)

173

what the bastard was up to.

"Burner and he's pinging it off different satellites. Don't know if he's doin' it or someone's doin' it for him, but I'd get Cassidy a new phone, brother. Keep the phone she has, but have one that the guy doesn't know about."

"Fuck!" I breathed out. "That's what I was afraid of. Cassidy said he's off to Paris and I have a feeling he's up to something."

"How much does he know about her?"

"Knowing Cass, not much. She's always been pretty tight-lipped when it came to her private life. He knows about me, though, and I'd imagine he knows who Maverick is, but outside of that, I have no fuckin' clue."

"So, he doesn't know that Maverick's father's in Paris?"

"Who the fuck knows? Cass left the father box on the birth certificate blank. Mack's workin' on the adoption paperwork, but it all fuckin' takes time."

"Okay, brother, we'll figure it out," Booker promised. "If the asshole's out of the country for a little while, it'll give us some time. My guy's callin' me tomorrow with an update."

I sighed. "I fuckin' hate this, Book."

"Yeah, I get it."

"Call me if you find anything, even if it's the middle of the night."

"I will, brother."

I hung up and climbed out of the truck. I'd kill anyone who got in my way and I knew that scared Cassidy, so I had to stow it.

* * *

Cassidy

Carter returned close to thirty minutes later and I watched him as he locked the door and took off his boots. The dog met him at the door just as excited as the first time he came in, so he gave her some love. I could tell he was trying to calm himself down. "I'm reheating your dinner, honey."

"Thanks," he said, and headed my way. He wrapped his arms around me and pulled me close, kissing my hair. "I'm gonna fuckin' kill him."

I squeezed him tight. "Don't, honey. I'm going to HR tomorrow to make a formal complaint. Either he'll be dealt with or I'll be fired, but either way, it'll be sorted."

"Why the fuck would they fire you?" he demanded.

I smiled up at him. "Because he's an executive and I'm a worker bee. Everyone knows HR's only there to cover the company's ass."

"Then just fuckin' quit!"

"No." I pulled away so I could grab his dinner from the microwave... again.

"Why the fuck not?"

"One, if I quit and he does this to someone else, I'll feel guilty, and two, if I quit, I won't get severance or unemployment. I don't have enough saved to just up and quit my job, Carter."

"I *do*, Cass. Walk out tomorrow and I'll take care of everything."

I frowned. "I like my job, honey. I like the people I work with... for the most part, it has great benefits and it's also in Vancouver, which means I don't have to pay income tax. Those jobs aren't easy to find right now."

He dragged his hands through his hair. "Cassidy, if you never wanted to work again, you wouldn't have to."

"Seriously?"

"Seriously," he said.

I bit my lip. "Well, that's good to know for the future, but right now, I'm young, I'm healthy, and I don't have a reason *not* to work, so I'd feel weird."

Carter stared at me but not for long. "If tomorrow doesn't go well, you quit."

"How about," I countered, looping my arms around his neck, "if Tom doesn't stop his unprofessional behavior, *then*

I quit? He might not fully understand how uncomfortable he's making me, and one word from HR will shut it down."

"I don't like it, Cass."

"I know, baby, but it'll be okay," I promised. "Why don't you eat and then we can do something fun?"

"Mav asleep?" he asked.

"Yep."

"Let's skip food," he said, leaning down to kiss me and lifting me so I could wrap my legs around his waist.

I smiled against his lips and slipped my hands in his hair as he carried me into the bedroom and closed the door. He lowered me to the mattress and tugged my shorts—panties and all—down my legs. God, I loved how he always started right here. Even if we weren't completely naked, he'd start with his face between my legs, and I'd forget about everything.

This time, however, he didn't spend as much time as he usually did. Don't get me wrong, I came and I came hard, but this was the first time I'd only come once before he was removing the rest of our clothes and sliding into me... and I loved it.

Ohmigod, this was definitely going on the approved list of sexual standard procedures.

"So fuckin' wet, baby."

"Yes!" I drew my knees up higher, wrapping my calves around his back. My ballet training gave me the ability to contort my body for optimum pleasure, and holy crap, tonight was most certainly optimum pleasure.

His mouth covered mine and his tongue slid into my mouth as he wrapped his big hand around my breast and squeezed. He rolled the nipple between his fingers as his hips surged into me, his tongue matching the motion with each thrust.

I lost his mouth on mine, but he moved his lips to my throat and I arched my neck to get more. "Drop a leg, baby."

I dropped a leg onto the mattress and mewed as he slid

176

his hand between us and fingered my clit. "Love my baby's cunt. Fuck, so tight and wet."

I tilted my hips and groaned. "Carter. Oh, God, I love you!"

"Come baby," he said, his breath coming in pants as he slammed into me again and again.

"More, honey."

He did as he was told and pressed in deeper and I exploded around him. He wasn't far behind and he collapsed on top of me, rolling us to our sides to keep our connection. I felt him pulse inside of me for several seconds and I wrapped my leg back around him. "Wow," I whispered.

He chuckled and kissed me. "Yeah, wow's good, babe."

I stroked his cheek and ran my thumb across his lower lip. "I had no idea."

"About?"

"How good this would be. Is it always like this?"

He nibbled gently on my thumb and shook his head. "It's never been like this for me."

"Liar." I narrowed my eyes.

"Never lied to you, Cassidy," he said, sounding a little irked.

I rolled my eyes. "You're telling me, that with the multitudes of women you've been with, you have never had sex this good?"

"That's exactly what I'm telling you."

"Seriously?"

"Seriously." Carter smiled. "There's a difference in making love and getting' off, and until you, it's been the latter."

I closed my eyes and smiled, wrapping my arms around his neck. "I love you so much it hurts sometimes."

Carter pulled me close and held me for a while before sliding out of me and making his way to the bathroom. He returned with a warm washcloth and cleaned me up, we dressed just enough in case Maverick came in during the night, and then I fell asleep in his arms, dinner and troubles forgotten.

* * *

The next morning, the alarm went off and I slammed my hand on the snooze button, rolling over with a smile and opening my eyes. What met my gaze had me squeaking and scrambling from the bed. Carter dropped his head back and laughed, patting the mattress. "Sorry, babe. I didn't mean to freak you out." He waved the tiny troll doll gently, complete with bright pink hair, and a diamond ring hanging from his arm. "Torbig and I have a question."

I shook my head as I climbed back into the bed. "You are ridiculous."

I bit my lip as Carter sat up and raised a knee. "Cassidy Eleanor Dennis, would you do me the great honor of marrying me?"

"Yes." I nodded, giggling as he slid the ring on my finger. It was exquisite. A huge oval diamond sat proudly between two smaller diamonds and the setting was intricate on both the top and sides with filigree that sparkled in the dim light. "Wow," I breathed.

"If you don't like it, baby, we can return it."

"It's perfect," I said, throwing my arms around him and kissing him. "Thank you."

He caught me and settled me across his chest.

"Maverick, you can come in now," Carter called.

Maverick shoved through the door and jumped on the bed. "Did you say yes, Mom?"

"I did say yes. But is that okay with you?"

"Carter's gonna be my dad, right?"

I grinned. "He is."

"Yes," Maverick exclaimed and pumped his fist in the air.

I laughed. "So you approve."

Maverick crossed his legs and nodded. "He already

asked me for permission, Mom."

"You did?" I asked Carter.

"Of course I did," he said. "I talked to your dad, too. Had to get the blessings from the two main men in your life."

I hugged his waist. "I love you."

"Are you guys gonna kiss now?" Maverick asked, a horrified expression on his face.

"Yeah, buddy," Carter answered.

"Gross. Can I please leave?"

"Sure thing," Carter said.

I giggled and dropped my head to Carter's shoulder. "Eat breakfast while I shower, please."

"Okay, Mom." Maverick left the bedroom, pulling the door closed behind him.

Carter kissed me, but not for long because my alarm sounded again. I groaned and broke the kiss. "I should get up."

"Or you could call in 'never coming back.'"

I giggled. "We have a good plan, honey. I'll call you after I talk to HR and we'll go from there."

"I'm going on record to say I still don't like the plan."

"I know."

"We're comin' to take you to lunch today, yeah? I need to get you a burner, so I'll bring that with me."

I sat up and turned off the alarm. "Why do I need a burner?"

"Because we blocked Tom's number and he still found a way to call you, so I want you to have a phone he doesn't know about."

I crossed my arms and frowned down at him, ignoring the overwhelming desire to lick his perfectly glorious chest from top to bottom. "Who is 'we'?"

"Club."

"Wait. You're telling me the club has access to my cell

phone?"

"No. Booker technically does, but Mack's workin' on some legal shit, so when I say the club, it encompasses those two... for now."

I gasped and widened my eyes in horror. "Does Booker have access to our texts?"

"No. Don't worry, babe. Those are just for us." Carter grinned. "He can probably access them, but I trust that he won't."

"Why did you just tell me that?" I grabbed a pillow and threw it at him. "Now I'm going to be beet red every time I see him!"

"Honey, he's a brother. I trust him. He won't access them without my permission, yeah?"

"No, Carter, it's not 'yeah'! Gah! This is humiliating." I stalked into the bathroom and started the shower. As I turned, I was pulled up against Carter and I sighed.

"I promise you, no one will see the texts. We can delete them now if it makes you feel any better," he said. "But they shouldn't embarrass you, baby. We're in love, we're gettin' married. It's an expression of how we feel—"

"A very, very graphic and *dirty* expression of how we feel," I grumbled.

He chuckled. "Fuck yeah, a very graphic and dirty expression of how we feel. How about I express a little bit more of my graphic and dirty feelings in the shower?"

"Make sure Maverick's okay and then you can have me for ten minutes."

"Start without me," he said, and left the room.

I took a moment to study my ring again and decided to shower with it on. I wasn't ready to take it off yet... I might never be.

Carter and Maverick dropped me off and, after sending an email to HR detailing everything that had happened with Tom, I went about getting through my To Do list. I was ahead of the curve for the moment, so when I got a call from Lana, our HR director, I was able to meet with her right away.

I headed to her office on the floor below me and closed the door.

EIGHTEEN

Ace

I TOOK MAVERICK with me to the club and found Hawk
had brought Lily, so I settled Maverick in the playroom
with her and my President's daughter, Ashley, who was
on kid watch duty for the day.

Since I hadn't talked to my brother in a while, I headed
to the office Hawk used to run his bounty hunter business
out of. Booker and Mack had offices as well, which kept the
club self-sufficient. I knocked.

"Come in," Hawk called.

"Hey," I said, and pushed the door open.

"Hey, man." Hawk turned from his computer and set his
feet up on the desk. "Heard someone's fuckin' with Cassidy."

"Yeah." I sat in one of the seats facing the desk. "Booker's dealin' with it right now. You workin' much this

week?"

"Got a couple assholes who jumped bail and went to ground. Got a lead on one, the other's a ghost."

Hawk was really good at his job. So good, in fact, he was paid accordingly. Two jobs a year could bring in as much as the average person's yearly salary, which afforded him the option of working when he wanted to, which was less now that he had Payton.

"What'd these guys do?"

Hawk slid the files toward me. "One's a drug dealer, beat a murder rap, got brought up on another one, convicted then released on a technicality. Got another murder rap, this one stuck and he ran. He's in Salem, so I'm headin' down there tonight."

"Shit."

"He's a dumb fucker, but he's a lucky dumb fucker."

"Sounds like it," I said.

"The other guy's slippery. Comes from money. Asshole who enjoys stalking and raping women. Two possible murders, but can't make them stick with no body."

I opened the file and my blood ran cold. "Fuck!"

"Yeah, he's a—"

"No, Hawk, this is the fucker who's messin' with Cassidy."

Hawk grabbed the file. "Seriously?"

"Yeah, seriously." I skimmed the file. "He said he was going to London and Paris."

"He's on a no-fly list, Ace. Don't know how he'd get out of the state, let alone the country."

"Fuck!" I stood and pulled open the door. "Watch Mav, yeah? I'm gettin' Cassidy."

"We got 'im, brother. I'll fill Booker in."

I nodded and headed to my bike. It'd be faster than my truck and I needed faster today.

Cassidy

I was leaving Lana's office when I was bombarded by Janie who was flailing her arms around in frantic, chicken-like movements. "You okay?" I asked.

"No," she squeaked. "Your boyfriend's in reception and he's freaking out. I think he has a gun, Cassidy."

I frowned. "Okay, I'll head there now."

As we walked toward the elevator bay, I felt a chill go up my spine, but the look on Janie's face made me sick to my stomach. I turned to see Tom with a crazed look on his face and a gun pointed at the two of us.

"Hello, Cassidy," he said. "I think it's time the two of us have a little talk."

"I'm sorry, Tom, but I need to get downstairs." Okay, probably not the right thing to say, but I'd never had a gun pointed at me before. I felt like talking him out of his plan might be a good option. I was wrong.

"You're not going anywhere." He turned the gun on Janie and shot.

She and I both screamed, and Janie fell to the ground. Before I could register the horror of watching someone get shot in front of me, I was yanked into a conference room and shoved against the table.

"Sit down, Cassidy," Tom ordered, and aimed the gun at me.

"Is Janie okay?" I asked, sobbing as I lowered myself in the chair.

"I need to explain some things to you. You're the one I want, Cassidy. You and I are going to get married and have children, and we'll live together in London." He waved his hands around as he spoke, and I was worried he'd shoot me. "You'll love England, sweetheart."

"Tom—"

"My name's not Tom!" he bellowed.

"It's not?"

"No! It's Robert."

I swallowed, nodding, trying to get my breathing under control. Who was this guy? As he stared at me with a hollow look on his face, all I could think about were Carter and Maverick. Why didn't I listen to Carter? He was right. I should never have come back to work.

"Say my name, Cassidy," he demanded.

"Robert," I rasped.

"As soon as it's clear—" Tom, or Robert, whoever he was, said "—we are going to walk out of here together. I will take you home and we can start our life."

"How—how will I get on a plane without a passport?" I asked.

"I have one for you."

I hiccupped, sobbing as I rubbed my arms, the fear suddenly making me cold. I caught movement through the window of the conference room door and tried to look somewhat covertly. Robert was watching me, his back to the door. I bit the inside of cheek to keep from crying out. Carter was there, although, I couldn't hear anything he was saying. I just had to trust that he had a plan and he'd protect me.

* * *

Ace

I had Lana, the HR director, pinned against the wall. "You fuckin' did this, lady, so you're not leavin' until my woman's out of that room and safe."

Another woman was kneeling beside the one who got shot, keeping pressure on the wound in her shoulder. It didn't look like it was life threatening, but I kind of wished it was. Fuckin' whore used Cassidy as a human shield. Bitch.

"I swear I knew nothing about him. It wasn't even my call," Lana cried.

185

"How the fuck did you people not know who he was? It's called a background check!"

"I don't know," she whispered. "I'm sorry. I don't know."

"Ambulance is on its way." I released her with a scowl. "You need to get these people out of the fucking building. Quietly. And when my people get here, you don't give them shit. They go wherever the fuck they want to go."

She nodded and rushed away from me, ushering people as quietly as she could to the stairs.

"Ace, what the fuck's goin' on?" Hawk demanded as he, Booker, Aidan, and our prez, Crow, walked toward him.

"Bastard's got Cassidy in that room," I said, waving the men to the wall out of sight.

Hawk nodded and pulled out his cell phone.

"What the fuck are you doin'?" I whispered.

"I'm callin' Brock," he said.

"Not gettin' into bed with the feds," Crow said.

"Trust me."

"Tell him to get Jax," I demanded, and Hawk nodded.

I honestly didn't much care who Hawk called. I just needed a clear shot of this fucker's head. So far, despite the glass, Robert never stayed within sight long enough for me to shoot.

* * *

Cassidy

"Tom—Robert, can we please talk about this," I begged. "I have a son. I can't just leave him and run away with you."

"We'll put him in boarding school and we'll have our own family, Cassidy," Robert said. He pulled a chair in front of me and smiled. "You'll see, sweetheart. I'll make you so happy."

"I can't live without my son, Robert."

"You were so beautiful," he continued, obviously not lis-

186

tening to me.

"What?"

"On the video call. I saw you sitting at the end of the conference table and I knew you were the one. I made them transfer me that day."

"I don't understand," I whispered.

"From the New York office." He frowned like I should know what he meant. "You remember the call, right?" I nodded. "When you were being introduced?"

"Exactly. I saw you and knew you were the one for me."

"But we don't know each other, Robert. There must be someone else who knows you—"

"No! It's you, Cassidy," he screamed. "It's always been you!"

He started waving the gun at me again and I raised my hand as some lame attempt to shield myself. "Okay, Robert. I'm sorry."

* * *

Ace

Jaxon slid the tiny camera under the crack of the conference room door and studied the screen at the end of it.

"Is she okay," I demanded.

"Yeah," Jaxon said. "The guy's sitting across from her, the gun's on his lap."

"Fuck!" I rasped. "It's been two hours, we need to get her out of there."

"Carter, I get it. But I need you to back up, so we can do our job."

* * *

Cassidy

I don't know how long I'd been in this room with Robert, but I was feeling stifled by the heat and the closeness of his

187

body, and I really had to pee.

The FBI had called into the phone in the room and all it managed to do was to make Robert even more frantic. I think he realized he wasn't walking out of here with me, and probably knew he'd be going away for a very long time.

"Robert, please. I could really use some water, and I'd like to talk to my son. Could we please just call them back?"

"Shut up!" He paced the room, his eyes and hands moving wildly.

"Please," I begged.

"You're not leaving this room, Cassidy. Just shut up."

"What do you mean?" I whispered.

"I'm not an idiot. I know there are agents outside waiting for us. I'm not leaving this room alive." He silenced me with a stare. "And neither are you."

* * *

Ace

A shot rang out, then a scream and another shot, and I shoved past my brother and into the conference room. "Cassidy! Somebody get the fuckin' paramedics in here now!"

Cassidy was slumped in a chair, blood pouring from her stomach. She had her hands over the wound, trying to keep pressure on it.

"Baby," I whispered, replacing her hands with mine. "I'm here. I've got you."

"He... he shot himself. In the head," she whispered, her eyes unable to focus on anything.

"I know, baby. Look at me. I've got you."

"It hurts."

"I know, honey. Help's coming." I turned and yelled, "Where the fuck are the paramedics?"

"Here," a young woman said and wheeled in a gurney, a large man following. "Sir, give us some space, please."

I found myself pulled away by Jaxon, and Cassidy was

lifted onto the gurney. The paramedics did whatever the fuck they did and then she was wheeled into the elevator. I followed, keeping hold of her hand, even though she'd passed out.

The rest of the day moved within a fog. I was forced to leave Cassidy in the hallway of the hospital as they wheeled her into emergency surgery. Most of the club arrived shortly after the ambulance did, along with Jaxon. Brock and Dallas were cleaning up and processing the crime scene.

An hour later, no one had given me any information and I was going crazy.

"Let me see what I can do," Macey offered. She had arrived with Payton and Dani, and happened to be an emergency room nurse in Portland. I highly doubted she'd have any access here, but I was desperate. I nodded and she left the group.

"Fuck," I whispered, dropping my still bloody hands on my head. "I have to get Maverick."

"He's fine," Payton said. "Ashley's got him and Lily totally entertained. She's ordering pizza and can stay with them all night if need be. We can also take him home later if you like."

Tears slipped down my face. "What do I tell him if she dies?"

"She's not going to die," Payton promised, wrapping an arm around my shoulders.

Jaxon sat in the chair next to me. "I called Cassidy's parents and Mia. Her mom will call Shannon and fill her in. They're on their way."

I nodded.

"I think you should get cleaned up," Jaxon said. "Aidan's grabbing you some clean clothes. I figured you wouldn't want to leave."

"Thanks."

Macey returned twenty minutes later and sat where Payton had been. "Dallas's brother called in privileges for me so

I could stay updated, but I can't give you any information without her next of kin's permission."

Dallas Stone was one of Jaxon's FBI partners, and Macey's husband.

"What the fuck?" I bellowed.

"I just need verbal approval from her mom or dad, Ace. Okay? If we can call them, then I should be covered."

"I'm on it." Jaxon pulled out his cell phone and dialed Cassidy's mother.

Once approval was given, Macey signed some forms, had me sign some forms, although I didn't read them, and then she left me again.

Macey became my personal liaison and I honestly didn't know how I would have managed without her. Aidan returned with clean clothes, and I took five minutes to go to the bathroom and wash up as best I could before shoving my dirty clothes, cut and all, in a plastic bag, and return to the waiting room.

Macey brought out a bag with Cassidy's belongings in it, but personally handed me her engagement ring. "I figured you probably wouldn't want this getting lost."

I nodded and pulled off the chain around my neck, slipping the ring onto it and sliding it back around my neck. I found Cassidy's matching chain and also slipped that around my neck.

"Surgery's going really well," Macey said. "They got the bleeding under control. She's out of the woods. I think they're just closing up really soon and then she'll go into the ICU for observation."

"But she's okay?" I asked.

"She's out of the woods."

I faced her with a frown. "That's not what I asked."

"Carter," Jaxon warned.

"Fuck off, Jax. I want her to tell me if Cassidy's okay."

"I really think you should wait for the doctor, so he can explain it."

"What aren't you telling me?" I demanded, shrugging off the hand that Jaxon placed on my shoulder.

Payton sat beside Macey and took her hand. "Just tell him, Mace."

Macey grimaced. "There was some damage to her uterine wall and they're concerned she may not be able to carry a baby."

"What?"

Macey nodded, her eyes filling with tears. She wiped them away quickly. "I don't know anything else. They called in OB/GYN and the doctor's an incredible surgeon, so I didn't want to panic you."

"Fuck!" I stood and paced the room. Everyone left me alone, which was wise.

NINETEEN

Ace

I WASN'T ABLE to see Cassidy for another two hours. She was resting comfortably, or so they said, but she was out, so I took her hand and raised it to my mouth, kissing her palm. I could do nothing but wait.

Her parents arrived an hour or so later and rushed into the room. After checking on Cassidy and kissing her cheek, Wendy wrapped me in a motherly hug. "Hi, honey."

I nodded and pulled away from her.

"Your friend Payton is going to take Maverick to her home and we've asked her not to say anything until we can explain to him what's going on."

"Thanks." I felt like the walls of the room were closing in on me, the panic rising suddenly and far too quickly.

"Son?" Patrick asked.

"I need a minute," I rasped, and stepped out of the room.

Bending at the waist, I anchored my palms on my thighs and took several deep breaths.

Visions of Cassidy being shot flew through my mind, only it was me doing the shooting... just like in my nightmares.

"Carter." Jaxon wrapped an arm around my shoulders and led me to a chair along the wall. "Take a beat."

"I did this," I whispered. "It's my fault."

"No, you didn't. You saw it comin' and got to her faster than anyone could. This could have gone much, much worse," Jaxon said.

"She might not be able to have any kids. That's on me," I argued. "I should have fuckin' tied her to a chair instead of lettin' her go into work."

"Look, I know nothing I say is gonna make you feel better, but you identified the threat and got to her faster than anyone could have. If you hadn't, he could have gotten her leaving the building and she might be somewhere you couldn't get to her. Trust me, brother, it could have been worse, and she's alive because of you."

I dragged my hands through my hair.

"Carter?" Wendy called. "She's asking for you."

I shot to my feet and made my way back to the room, stepping to the bed. "Hey, baby."

"Where's Maverick?" she asked.

"He's with Payton, honey. He's safe."

"I want him here," she said, grabbing my hand and squeezing. "Please, bring him here. I need to see him."

"Okay, baby. I'll get Hawk to bring him."

"Don't leave."

I smiled, leaning down to kiss her gently. "I'm gonna have Jax tell Hawk. I'll be right back."

"He's okay?"

"He's great, baby. I promise. No one's told him anything."

"Wait," she said. "Maybe we shouldn't tell him yet."

"Whatever you want me to do, I'll do it, honey." Cassidy still hadn't released my hand.

"We should probably wait."

I kept hold of her hand as I sat in the chair next to the bed.

"Are you in any pain, honey?" Wendy asked.

"Not right now," Cassidy said. "Everything just feels kind of tight."

Wendy fussed while Patrick sat on the other side of her, his hand on her arm like he was afraid she'd disappear. Two doctors walked in a few minutes later and closed the door.

"I'm Dr. Nelson," the surprisingly young, attractive female surgeon said.

"I'm Dr. Waring," the older man with her said.

"Perhaps we should get some privacy, so we can talk," Dr. Nelson said.

"I'm fine," Cassidy said. "They can stay."

I linked my fingers with hers. I had an idea of what was coming and knew she'd have a difficult time processing.

"There was quite a bit of internal damage, which we were able to repair, however, we are still concerned about the damage to your uterus."

Cassidy gasped. "What happened to my uterus?"

"The bullet damaged the uterine wall and I was afraid I'd have to perform a hysterectomy."

"Did you?" Cassidy asked, tears sliding down her face. I kissed her hand, laying her hand against my cheek.

"No. I repaired what I could," Dr. Nelson said. "But only time will tell if there will be any further complications. It's possible you might not be able to carry another child, Cassidy."

"What?" Cassidy burst into tears.

"We don't know for sure yet, honey," I said.

"But you want a hundred kids," she cried.

"There are other ways to get kids, baby," I whispered, stroking her cheek.

"It's not a definite outcome," Dr. Nelson said. "We have every hope that your body will do what it's designed to do and finish off the healing process. We'll keep a close eye on you and monitor you as you heal."

I watched as Cassidy shut down. I knew it the second her tears stopped, and she started nodding at everything the doctors said. She'd checked out and wasn't listening to anything they were saying. I did my best to focus on the doctor's instructions because she'd need to know eventually.

* * *

Cassidy was sleeping and Patrick was making a food run while Wendy quietly read a book, so I stepped into the hallway to call Hawk.

"Hey, Ace."

"Hey. Cass has to be here for at least a week, so I'm thinkin' I'll come pick up Maverick tomorrow and bring him, if that's okay."

"No problem. We told him you and Cassidy were doin' somethin' so he got to stay the night with us. He's happy, man. We got him."

I sighed. "Thanks. 'Preciate it."

"You wanna talk to him?"

"No, because he might want to talk to Cass and she's asleep."

"Good thinkin'. Okay, just swing by tomorrow whenever. We'll be here."

"Thanks again." I hung up and made my way back into the room, interrupting an argument between Cassidy and her mother. "What's goin' on? You okay?"

"Fine." Cassidy glared at her mom.

"Hey," I said, and sat beside her again. "What's up?"

"She thinks you two should break up," Wendy provided.

"*Mom*," Cassidy snapped.

"Why?" I asked carefully.

"Because she's decided that what's done is done and

195

since she can't give you children, she's useless to you," Wendy said.

"Mom, shut *up!*" Cassidy hissed.

I stood and smiled. "Wendy, can I have a few minutes with your daughter?"

"Only if you plan to talk some sense into her."

"Of course I do."

Wendy smiled, kissed my cheek, and sidled out the door. I went back to the bed, but instead of sitting on the chair, I sat on the mattress beside Cassidy.

"We don't have to make any decisions now," Cassidy whispered, not meeting my eyes.

"Look at me, Cassidy," I demanded quietly.

Her eyes flew to me and I raised her palm to my lips. "I'm not goin' anywhere."

"I know you say that now because I'm lying—"

"I swear to fuckin' Christ, Cassidy, you keep talkin' like that and I will handcuff you permanently to this bed. You'll be stuck with me literally."

"You don't own handcuffs," she grumbled.

"Yes, I do."

"You do?"

I nodded.

"Do I want to know why you have those handcuffs?" she asked.

"It's not because of anything fun," I informed her. "Look, this sucks. All of it. But we're in it together and if you talk about us doin' anything goin' forward alone, I will lose my fuckin' mind. I don't love you because you can or can't give me kids. I love you and Maverick with every part of me, and you are enough. You're more than enough. If we want more kids and we can't get them the traditional way, then we'll adopt or use a surrogate, or whatever."

"But you want a *lot* of kids."

"You're not hearin' me, honey," I said. "I want you more than I want more kids, Cassidy. I've tried livin' without you.

196

It doesn't work and if you try to separate me from our kid, you'll regret it."

"Dipshit bolt." I could tell she was trying not to smile.

"Fuckin' nut," I retorted.

"I'm giving you an out, Carter."

"Fuck me, Cass, I don't want an out." I pulled our chains from around my neck and helped her put hers on, before pulling her engagement ring off my chain and sliding it back onto her finger. "You're my world, baby. I can't live without you. Either of you."

I leaned down to kiss her, but she turned her head. "I haven't brushed my teeth since this morning."

"I don't care," I said, and kissed her. After breaking the kiss, I stroked her cheek. "I'm gonna get your mom. No more talk of us breaking up, yeah?"

"Okay," she whispered.

"I talked to Hawk and I'll pick Maverick up and bring him tomorrow. Tonight he'll stay blissfully unaware that anything's wrong, yeah?" She nodded, her face contorting in pain. "How bad?"

"Bad, but…" she said, and pressed the button for the pain pump, quickly falling asleep.

TWENTY

Cassidy

ONE WEEK LATER, I arrived home to find my apartment spotless, organized, and filled with flowers. There were enough meals to feed the three of us for over a month, and my parents were staying in town for another two weeks to help.

I would have limited mobility for several more weeks, but it didn't worry me because, not only did I never have to go back to work again, the company was covering all of my medical bills and Mack was working on a settlement which would set us all up for life. Admittedly, it was a really shitty way to get set up for life, but I was alive and I was grateful.

We'd managed to fill Maverick in on as much as we could without completely freaking him out, but he was a smart kid and he didn't like to see me in pain, so he hovered a lot. I was glad it was summer so that he could just hang out with me and watch me heal. He wouldn't have done well if he'd had to go to school every day and function.

Something I hadn't been prepared for were the nightmares. I would relive the incident over and over again, several times a night, and I hadn't slept well in quite a while.

A few days after I arrived home, I was planted in the recliner my dad had bought since it was too painful to stretch out flat, and Carter walked in from walking the dog. Maverick was on the sofa and we were watching a movie. "Hi, honey," I said.

"Hey." Carter leaned over to kiss me. "Do you need anything?"

I shook my head with a smile. "Mav's got it covered."

The pain was beginning to get worse, but I wanted to try to wean myself off the narcotics, so I tried to wait longer each time.

Carter sat next to him. "Thanks, buddy."

"No problem."

"You okay?" I asked.

Carter nodded. "Yeah. Just got a weird phone call."

"Weird good or weird bad?"

"Good," he said.

"Club business?"

Carter shook his head. "The house next door to Hawk's is for sale."

I widened my eyes. "The cute little blue one with the basement?"

"That's the one."

"And?"

"Wondered if you wanted to buy it," Carter said.

I gasped. "Seriously?"

"Yeah, babe."

"But what about your house?"

"Aidan can rent it from me. Or buy it if he wants it. He's open."

I blinked back tears. "You'd do that for us?"

"Babe," he said with a sigh. "I'm not sacrificin' anything. I like it up here and Mav's already in school right down the street. We'd be close to a brother, and you'd be close to Payton. It's an ideal situation."

I grinned. "Hunt and gather, man of mine. I want that house."

He laughed and nodded. "I'm lookin' at it tomorrow. If I like what I see, then you can check it out and we'll make it happen."

"Can I come with you, Dad?" Maverick asked.

I laid my hand over my chest. It was the first time Maverick had called Carter 'dad,' and it was precious.

"If your grandma can come hang out with Mom, then yeah, of course you can. Maybe Grandpa can come too," Carter said.

"Awesome!" Maverick sat up on his knees. "Does that mean I get to live next to Lily?"

"If we buy the house, yep, that's what it means."

"Cool," he said. "Now that Dad's home, can I please play on my DS?"

"Yeah, honey. Thirty minutes," I said.

"Okay." Maverick scrambled from the sofa and headed to his room.

Carter checked his watch and rose to his feet. "You're due for meds, babe."

"Oh, good," I said, the pain getting stronger with each minute. "I hope this doesn't go on forever. I feel really great for a while and then it just hits."

"I know, baby," Carter said, and grabbed my pills.

I took them and smiled up at him. "I'm okay, honey."

"I know that here—" he tapped his temple, "but here—" he laid his hand over his heart, "I don't like it."

"I get it."

He leaned over me, bracing his hands on each arm of my chair. "If you really got it, Cassidy, you'd quit waiting longer for relief."

I sighed. "I was hoping you hadn't noticed that."

"I notice everything when it comes to you."

"I'm picking up on that," I admitted. "I just don't want to get addicted."

"Cassidy, you were *shot* less than ten days ago. You got a whole lotta time before you run the risk of getting addicted. Take the damn pills."

I reached up and stroked his cheek. "Okay, honey. I'll take the pills."

"Thank you." He leaned in and kissed me quickly, then rose to his full height. "Can you eat somethin'?"

"I could try. Something small, though."

He smiled. "Okay, babe. I'll find you something."

Carter fixed dinner and the three of us ate together in front of a movie.

* * *

Six weeks later, despite the fact I wasn't allowed to lift a finger, the three of us moved into our new house next to Hawk and Payton. It was perfect. The top floor was a ranch style with three bedrooms, two and a half bathrooms, an office, huge kitchen and great room, and a basement with another two bedrooms, a bathroom, a kitchenette and a bonus room that Carter wanted to convert into a media room.

I could never have imagined living somewhere so nice, not on my salary and living as a single mother, but as I watched (from my place on the recliner in the great room) the club and my family carrying in boxes and furniture while I sipped water and directed the flow, I realized the dreams I had so long ago were happening right in front of me. They might have taken a little longer than I expected, but they were no less sweet.

We'd been married now for two weeks. Our ceremony took place at the courthouse as Carter had suggested at the beginning (with Torbig in attendance, but not presiding over the event). However, Carter made up for the low-key event by making the club organize a major party. We'd have to postpone our honeymoon due to my health issues, but I was happy to bask in the glow of him for the moment, the honeymoon could wait a few months. Within all of the drama, Maverick celebrated his birthday, and he was happy that we'd rented out Chuck-E-Cheese for the day and filled it with club kids and friends from school. He *loved* being the center of attention.

Carter had made the difficult decision to cut ties once and for all with his mother. He left the door open, but there were specific stipulations to her being let "back in." And the biggest one was that she had to accept me completely, which right now, she wasn't ready to do. I would have tried, but Carter said that I shouldn't have to. She was the one with the problem, so she had to be the one to fix it. Again, he was protecting me, and again, I let him, because the alternative wasn't particularly pleasant. I didn't want to be at family gatherings and feel as though I wasn't welcome.

A surprising friendship with Josh's wife, Melanie, had come out of Carter's ultimatum to his mother, and I found Mel to be warm and giving, and extremely funny. But she'd been the first to deal with Sheila's passive aggressive nastiness, and had borne the brunt of all of it. Melanie had confided in me that she hoped Josh would stand up to Sheila one day, but until then, she would live vicariously through me.

As I sat in my recliner and guided traffic, I decided supervising was fun, especially while relaxing and being fussed over by my man in between him utilizing his gorgeous muscles to move heavy stuff. Yum.

I knew that it would take some time to come to terms with not having Carter's children, but he was right, life apart was torture, but together we could face anything. So, I settled in and took my man's advice, to not worry so much. I had been blessed beyond measure and it was more than enough.

EPILOGUE

Cassidy

Two years later…

"I DON'T UNDERSTAND," I said as I stood on the phone with the doctor. I'd been dealing with the stomach flu for weeks now, and Carter had forced me to go in and find out what the hell was going on.

"Well, Mrs. Quinn, you don't have the stomach flu. You're pregnant."

"But that's impossible."

"Well, if this isn't good news, I can refer you to someone you can talk to."

"No," I rushed to say. "It's not that. It's just I was shot, and the doctor said I wouldn't be able to have children. Are you sure you're right? Maybe I should come in and take another test."

The truth was, it hadn't been definite, but considering we hadn't used any kind of birth control since I'd been released from the hospital, my OB/GYN hadn't been particularly positive that a pregnancy would happen. We'd resigned ourselves to not having a baby the natural way... well, until now apparently.

"We ran both blood and urine tests, so there's no mistake. I think we should schedule you for an ultrasound, so we can check things out at this early stage, but you're definitely pregnant."

I shook my head in disbelief.

"Mrs. Quinn?"

"Sorry, I'm here," I said. "Um, yes, let's schedule the ultrasound."

The nurse transferred me to the scheduling desk and I took the earliest appointment available before hanging up the phone and promptly rushing to the bathroom to throw up again.

As I sat on the floor of our powder room, I couldn't stop myself from giggling uncontrollably. Of course I was pregnant. Being married to Carter Quinn ensured it, considering he probably had bionic sperm and made every problem his bitch. A little thing like my uterus being shot to hell was nothing he couldn't "fix."

Because we tended to go at it like rabbits, I couldn't really estimate when it had happened, but I didn't care. If I could carry this baby to term, it meant we could have more and I wanted more. It was long past time Maverick had a sibling.

"Babe!" Carter called, and I heard the garage door close.

"In here."

He pushed open the door and frowned, hunkering down beside me. "You sick again?"

"Yeah, but—"

"Has that fuckin' doctor called you back yet?" He stood and rinsed a washcloth with cold water, laying it gently on my forehead. "I'm gonna call them and find out why the fuck they haven't figured out what's wrong."

"They have, honey. I just got off the phone with them."

He knelt beside me again, his face pale and his expression grave. "Tell me."

"I'm pregnant." Yep, I just spit it out. No easing into the information, just dropped the bomb.

"Come again."

I giggled, but stopped myself from giggling like a loon... sort of. "I'm pregnant. I'm going in the day after tomorrow for an ultrasound."

"Pregnant."

"Yep."

"You're gonna have my baby," he whispered.

"Well, no, it's the gardener's baby, but I'd hoped to wait to tell you that information for a while."

He rolled his eyes and cupped my face. "Holy fuck, a baby."

I nodded. "Yep."

He rose to his feet. "What do you need? I'll run to the store and get saltines and lemon-lime soda. What about juice? Can you handle juice?"

"We have all that stuff now. I think I'm set for a while." I stood as well and brushed my teeth quickly.

"You should go to bed."

"Honey, I'm fine. If this pregnancy is anything like what I had with Maverick, I'll be feeling totally great in a few weeks. My pregnancy with him was a breeze."

Carter laid his hand gently on my stomach. "Will you at least sit in the recliner and relax for now? We'll go to the ultrasound and decide what to do from there."

I looped my arms around his neck. "If you want me to sit in the recliner and let you serve me for the next two days, I won't argue, but I really need you not to worry."

"Look who's changed positions."

I grinned. "We're gonna have a hundred kids, Carter. I have to learn not to stress out every second."

He leaned down and kissed me. "I love you, Cassidy Eleanor Quinn."

"I love you too, honey."

"In the chair."

I laughed and let him lead me to the recliner where he fussed over me until Maverick got home from school. Then they both did. Saying that Maverick was excited about a sibling was an understatement, although, he'd just gone through his health class at school, so he was both excited and grossed out. After all, Payton was close to having her new little boy, so it was incredible to me that we'd be raising our kids together.

Later that night, Carter took me to bed and made love to me gentler than he ever had, which at one time, I thought would bore me, but I decided this was definitely going on the approved list of sexual standard procedures.

Seven months later, Liam Patrick Quinn arrived. The boy we affectionately called "Moose," weighed in at nine pounds, eight ounces and was twenty-two inches long. It was no wonder I'd looked like a Volkswagon Beetle while carrying him.

As I held our second son in my arms, I kissed Carter and smiled. "Thank you for forgiving me."

"Aw, baby, I was just going to say the same thing." He kissed Liam, pulled Maverick onto the bed with us and hugged him. "I love you guys."

"Love you too, Dad," Maverick said.

"Love you, honey."

He kissed me again and I snuggled up against my family, basking in the joy of the miracle and healing of absolution.

Life was perfect.

ABOUT PIPER

Piper Davenport is the alter-ego of *New York Times Bestselling Author*, Tracey Jane Jackson. She writes from a place of passion and intrigue, combining elements of romance and suspense with strong modern-day heroes and heroines.

She currently resides in the Pacific Northwest with her author husband and two kids.

Like Piper's FB page and get to know her!
(www.facebook.com/piperdavenport)

Made in the USA
Coppell, TX
24 March 2022

75468742R00125